NIGHT FIRE
Nightriders MC #3

_____

Silver James

Contact: silverjames@swbell.net

Cover design © by *Clary Carey*, clarycarey@gmail.com
Images: www.depositphotos.com
Sexy Santa with present ©citylights
Motorcycle in flames ©3quarks
Wolf jump illustration ©I.Petrovic

Edited by Gregory Alan

First Print, United Sates of America 2019
ISBN-13: 978-0-9969994-8-9
9 8 7 6 5 4 3 2 1

DEDICATION

To everyone who has ever lived
vicariously through a book.

ACKNOWLEDGEMENTS

Writing is the one profession where the voices in my head mean I'm not totally bat-shit crazy when I talk back to them. I love my voices, even when they argue with me. Which they do. Way more than they should. Silly buggers.

As always, many thanks to my readers, the Facebook crew at Silver James Romance, friends, and family.

I truly appreciate the help I receive from my critique partner Heidi, beta reader Siobhan, and cover artist Clary for the many "do-overs" until we get things right. I couldn't do what I do without the help and guidance of my wonderful husband aka Lawyer Guy. Last but definitely not least, I want to recognize the fans of each of my series. Each email, Facebook comment, tweet, and visit to my website convinces me that the Wolves, Nightriders, Hard Target Team, and denizens of the Penumbra Papers all deserved to see the light of day.

One last caveat: Any and all mistakes are my own.

FIRE

Smoke

THE WORLD goes still in those moments between night and sunrise. The weak—human or animal—know they haven't survived the long hours of dark, not yet. They are prey, especially when the biggest predator of all is prowling. I hunt for a living. More precisely, I do whatever the fuck the Russian tells me to do. At the moment, I was tracking the idiots stupid enough to take on the Nightriders.

The glow in the west was a man-made dawn. Fire. I like fire. A lot. It's a living, breathing supernatural entity. You can tease it. Taunt it. Tame it. You can love it. And damned if I didn't. For the unwary, Fire is a dangerous mistress but I've made her my own for years now.

The Russian sent me down here to Dallas to do a job. Daylight wasn't burning but the evidence was. Here in the gray light of dawn, I dropped all pretense of humanity. Reaching for my wolf, I let him roam free. Damn but it felt good.

ONE

Leigh

I DIDN'T HATE the dark. Not really. But driving down a two-lane road on the industrial outskirts of Dallas at 4:00 a.m. on a cold autumn morning was not on my list of Top 10 Fun Things To Do On The Job. At least I hadn't been up all night putting out the warehouse fire. Nope. They waited to call me until I'd finally snuggled under my down comforter after being up most of the night at the scene of a suspicious house fire. I made a mental note to check my sarcasm at the crime scene tape once I got there. The guys wouldn't appreciate it.

Fog swirled in front of my headlights and I wished, not for the first time, that I'd driven my POV instead of the department's POS. Personally Owned Vehicles were infinitely better than Pieces Of Shit. At least mine was. My Toyota Highlander had fog lamps and four-wheel drive. The arson squad's sedan was over ten years old and its headlights barely penetrated the dark.

A shadow darted across the road right in front of me. Animal. I slammed on the brakes, fought the vehicle as its tires grabbed the asphalt. A thump. The car shuddered. Tires lost traction as wheels locked. And then I was holding on for dear life as the POS bounced off the road, careened across the rough-grade shoulder while a kaleidoscope of light and dark spun around me. It stopped. Finally.

I took a breath. Slowly released the steering wheel and blood returned to my fingers. Had I hit the dog? The red Dallas Fire Department sedan listed to one side, nose down in the bar ditch. Unbuckling, I pushed the door open and leveraged myself out, stepped back about five feet and bit back a string of curse words. There was no way I'd be able to drive out the ditch.

I reached into the front seat to snag my handheld radio and the door banged against the back of my thighs. Ow! This time, I said all those curse words aloud. No one was around to hear. I should have been on the fire scene twenty minutes ago. The guys from Station 51 had been standing around in the creepy fog waiting for me. Before I could radio Dispatch, the roar of a big motorcycle echoed in the miasma. Moving further from the roadbed, I watched the ghostly bike appear, roar past, and then disappear.

Except it didn't. The motorcycle reappeared through the misty dark, driving the wrong way back toward me on the shoulder. As an arson investigator, I'm cleared to carry a sidearm, but guns are not my thing. I always counted on my colleagues and the cops for backup if there was a situation where a weapon might be needed.

I was totally regretting that decision now.

The guy tossed his leg over his Harley and stalked toward me. He was six feet four inches and 230 pounds of do whatever the hell he wanted. His dark, shaggy hair had been combed by the wind. His eyes, color to be determined, were hooded. Fog drifted between us, almost as thick as smoke and then he was there, suddenly, feet braced, massive arms crossed over his chest, black leather jacket stretched to capacity.

"Having trouble?"

Great. The guy was a master of the understatement, not to mention that if his name was Trouble, I wouldn't mind having some. Wait. What was I thinking? I flicked one hand toward the car. "You could say that."

His gaze raked over me—down, up, down, then it zeroed in on my chest for an uncomfortable moment before coming to rest on my face. I'd pulled on a pair of very serviceable coveralls, black combat-style boots, and a department baseball cap when I rolled out of bed. Sexy, for sure. Not.

"You a cop?"

"No. Fire department."

"No station out this way." He stepped closer.

I backed up. "I think I hit a dog." I wanted to give myself a head slap. Talk about a *non-sequitur*.

♟ ♟ ♟ ♟

Smoke

THERE WAS NO *thinking* about it. Her front bumper had clipped me and it took real focus not to limp as I approached. I resisted rubbing my thigh despite the burning ache. She was really something, even hiding in those shapeless navy coveralls. My nose detected the sweet-cherry residue from a house fire and I could read her patches even in the semi-dark. Dallas Fire Department. Arson squad. Fuck.

She raised her chin, pretending she wasn't jumpy. The stink of scalded milk curled around the cherry wood. Yup. I made her nervous. Good. I knew where she was headed. I'd just left there. I needed to find out how good she was at her job.

"What's your name?"

She crossed her arms over a very nice rack. "Sergeant Daniels."

Smart ass. I liked that in my women. Even if she was the investigator on this fire, I was definitely gonna make her mine for the duration.

"What's your first name?"

"None of your business."

"Can I call you None for short?"

"Smart ass."

Yeah, takes one to know one. She'd muttered it under her breath but I'm a Wolf. I hear better than the average bear and a hellava lot better than a human.

"What about you?"

"What about me?"

"What's your name?"

"Smoke."

"What kind of name is that?"

"My kind of name."

I caught her studying the patches on my cut and considered turning around so she could see my full patch. I'm a Nightrider, out of our original chapter in Kansas City, but I ride all over so my bottom rocker says *Nomad*. I work directly for the Russian, our national president. He's the one who bestowed my road name. Anymore, that's the only name I need. My existence ended and my real life started the day I patched in to the club.

"Is that like a nickname?"

"No. It's my road name."

"Road name. So…you *do* belong to one of those motorcycle gangs." She sneered, lip curled, nose crinkled. Like a cat trying to look all tough.

"We aren't a gang. We're a club." We were more but I wasn't about to discuss brotherhood or pack with her, no matter how good she smelled and how fuckable she looked.

"Look, I'm en route to a fire scene. You're wasting my time."

I leaned to peer around her, gave her a look. That heap in the ditch wasn't going anywhere except onto a rollback wrecker.

"You won't get anywhere in a hurry in

that piece of shit. You broke the rear axle."

She huffed out a breath hard enough it ruffled her bangs under that ball cap. I pointed to her radio. "Call a wrecker. I'll give you a ride to your scene."

Sergeant None of Your Business Daniels worked her mouth like she wanted to form words. None came out but those lips sure put ideas into my head. My dick liked those ideas. A lot.

I gave her about a minute, then turned around and walked away. "Suit yourself."

Took her five seconds to yell, "Wait!"

Keeping my back to her, I did. I heard her rummaging around in the wrecked car. She called her dispatch, using the typical radio speak cops and first responders liked so much. As soon as she said she was leaving the car and heading on to the scene, I started walking. At my bike, I swung a leg over, kick-started it, and waited. She had a backpack slung over one shoulder and was chewing her lips. Damn if my dick and balls didn't want to come out to play.

"I got places to be, and it ain't out here in the middle of fuckin' nowhere. Get on the bike, babe."

"I'm not your *babe*."

"Ain't my sergeant either. Name, babe."

"Leigh."

"See? That wasn't so hard. Get on, hang on."

She did.

TWO

Smoke

I WATCHED LEIGH climb through the rubble. Acrid smoke curled in tendrils from various points around the scene. Not much left of the building. Which was good because the authorities wouldn't know what had been stored there. Bad because the place had been full of contraband and someone had gone to a lot of trouble to make it look like it belonged to the Nightriders. Except it wasn't ours, despite all the clues linking the local club to that shit.

Ignoring the cop glaring at me, his hand cocked on his sidearm, I leaned against a fire engine waiting for Leigh to finish her preliminary investigation. She was nothing if not thorough. Almost an hour later, she approached two of the firefighters.

"Captain Slattery," she greeted and nodded at the older guy. Whipcord lean, I figured he didn't take shit from anyone. Good to know.

With in-born stealth, I shifted a little closer to hear their conversation.

"...multiple ignition points, and in places that guaranteed complete collapse." Leigh shoved her hands into the hip pockets of her coveralls. Frustration, as bitter and sulfurous as a striking match, rolled off her. My palms itched. Damn but I wanted to do the same fucking thing as her hands, cupping that sweet ass. Business first though. I'd made sure the contraband was ash, but I needed to stick close to the investigation. My wolf just laughed his ass off. He knew it was Leigh that interested me.

"Place has been empty for years," a guy wearing lieutenant's rank and a name tag that read "Wills" said. "There's been a few attempts at renovation in the last couple of years and a work crew was out here a few weeks ago."

Leigh shook her head and opened her mouth, but Slattery spoke first. "You don't believe this could have been an accident?"

"No, sir. It wasn't. I'll need to collect samples and send them to the state lab, but in my opinion, this is arson. And a professional job. The warehouse wasn't empty."

Fuck. Leigh Daniels was a damn good arson investigator. She was also damn sexy, as my dick reminded me with a hard twitch. As if she knew I was thinking about her, she sought me out with a narrowed glare.

"Why are you still here?" she yelled.

Yeah, sexy as hell. And mean too. My kind of woman. I offered her a sardonic grin designed to piss her off. "I figured you needed a ride home," I called back.

"Get lost! I'll catch a ride with the

captain."

"Nope. I brought you to this dance, I'll be the one taking you home."

Her upper lip curled and I swore I could hear her teeth grind just beneath the sound of the guttural snarl she favored me with. I laughed, which only pissed her off even more. Yeah, chasing and catching Leigh Daniels was going to be a lot fun. Ironic that she'd be hunting me at the same time. Fun times.

🐾 🐾 🐾 🐾

Leigh

Trying to concentrate with the sexy biker hanging around was frustration squared. It didn't help that my guys kept giving him the fisheye and the cops looked like they wanted to take him down to the ground and handcuff him.

Someone yelled and a moment later, what was left of the front exterior wall collapsed. Slattery took off to assess the situation and Wills nudged me. His gaze was pinned on the biker as he said, "Bad news walkin', sugar."

"Don't need to tell me twice, Willsy." Since we'd gone through the academy together, I let his name-calling slip. This once at least.

"So what're you doing with him, Leigh? I mean, seriously."

I was embarrassed about wrecking my

department sedan, but I needed to 'fess up so we could move on. "Dog ran across the road. Like an idiot, I put my department ride in the ditch. He showed up, offered me a lift. I knew y'all were sitting on your thumbs waiting for me to get here."

He waggled his finger at me. "Didn't we teach you better? No riding with strangers."

I heartily agreed but... I watched Smoke over Wills' shoulder. I didn't know the guy...but I did. Getting on that bike? Putting my hands on his waist? It was like *déjà vu* all over again. Touching him made me think of hot, sweaty nights and naked skin. I'd never reacted to any man that way. Was I freaked out by it? Totally!

Wills had continued talking but I didn't tune back in until I heard him say, "I'll have the cops run him off."

Wait, what? I tilted my head, speculating about the possibilities. Yeah, no. Smoke was dangerous, and I didn't want anyone to get hurt. I did my best to pretend that the police could take him, but I had a deep-seated feeling that wasn't the case. The freaking man exuded power and menace—at least toward every man on scene. Me? I'd never felt safer and wasn't that the craziest thought ever.

"No."

Eying me with concern, Wills tried again. "Look, if he's bothering—"

"He's not."

"Don't you dare say he's harmless."

I almost doubled over laughing. "He's about as harmless as a pit full of pissed off rattlesnakes." Or a rabid wolf. I sucked in air. Stopped breathing for a few seconds. Yeah. A wolf. That's what Smoke reminded me of. I shook myself mentally and physically.

"Look, y'all still have to finish off the hot spots and break down equipment. I need to check on the wrecker and head to the office to write my report. I have my radio with me. I'll be fine."

"Leigh," Wills cautioned, but I ignored him. I strode towards Smoke, watching him, weighing his reactions. I was a trained investigator. And this guy was full of secrets.

"I need five minutes," I told Smoke when I stopped in front of him. His smile was full of conceit—and knowledge, like he'd been positive I'd acquiesce to his wishes. Heck, who was I kidding. Wishes had nothing to do with it. He'd *commanded* me and here I was.

"Long as it takes, babe." He smirked at Wills and the cops.

I rolled my eyes and headed toward the captain. "At ease, boy," I called over my shoulder. His velvet-rough chuckle made things heat up low in my center.

Giving a brief verbal report to Captain Slattery, with assurances that I'd copy him on the report, took about five minutes. Smoke was already on his Harley when I got back. Nobody on the inside of the crime scene tape seemed happy to see me duck under and climb on the back.

Smoke took off as my hands gripped his sides. A few minutes later, we passed the spot where I'd wrecked. The sedan was gone. More paperwork. I leaned forward and yelled above the wind. "I need to go—"

Smoke cut me off. "I know where you need to go."

THREE

Smoke

MY WOLF WANTED OUT. Hell, *I* wanted out. I've never liked cities and the Dallas/Ft. Worth metroplex was a big one. Still, I wasn't about to let Sergeant Leigh Daniels out of my sight. Figuratively speaking. She'd been inside the cinder-block building masquerading as the arson squad HQ since I'd dropped her off about 6:30 a.m. I'd found a spot where I could watch both the front and the back.

Squinting up at the sun, I figured noon wasn't too far off. My stomach grumbled. Wolves have fast metabolisms and the animal needs to be fed. Often. My wolf agreed, but he was hungry for the woman. Me too. There was something about her that drew both sides of my nature. My wolf side was embedded in my DNA. Literally. Wolves carry a little extra *somethin-somethin* on our Y chromosome. The scientific types call it the *lupi versi pellis* gene. Wolf shifters, not werewolves. We have better senses, can heal a bit faster but scars stay and bullets can kill. They don't have to be silver.

We aren't magic. We're just...

preternatural. And we tend to be adrenaline junkies. Goes with the territory. My wolf abruptly stopped pacing and came to attention. We both focused on the rear exit door across the street. Leigh came out, talking to a couple of guys and a girl who looked about twenty. Co-workers but the wolf didn't like males anywhere near her. He wanted to go to her. I needed to wait, tucked back here in the mid-day shadows of the alley.

Playing my hand too early was a bad idea. I reminded the wolf of that. He wasn't happy but he settled down so I could concentrate. The males got into separate shit-red vehicles while Leigh and the kid kept walking. Evidently, the department hadn't replaced her duty vehicle. But who was the girl?

They cut around the chain-link fence and headed toward the busy street fronting the building. I made a snap decision and stripped. I called up my wolf and gritted my teeth against the twisting-tearing that signified the change. It hurt like a sumbitch. Even so, I had an easier time with the change than a lot of Wolves. Few could do it as quickly and seamlessly as I could, despite the pain.

Trying to look like a shaggy German Shepherd, I trotted across the street and tracked Leigh. I turned the corner and found the two women a block ahead of me, walking steadily toward a bus stop. I ducked behind a delivery truck when Leigh glanced back over her shoulder. I waited until the bus came and the women boarded. I'd be able to track it.

Five minutes later, I was idling half a block behind the bus. A couple of young guys admired the bike. An old dude snarled. I snarled back. He slunk down in the seat of his car.

Start and stop. People on. People off. Leigh and the girl were sitting four seats back from the driver. The bus wove through Dallas, steadily heading north and east. The girl got off close to SMU. College student, I decided. Probably an intern. She walked about a block and ducked into the coffee shop on the corner.

The riders thinned out and the bus traveled steadily now. Where the hell did Leigh live? We crossed under I-635, still going north. The bus started stopping again, people getting off. Three stops in, Leigh emerged. She slung her backpack and trudged up the street as the bus groaned away in a puff of noxious diesel smoke.

I circled around then hung back. As long as she was on foot, I'd be able to track her. Even with all the car exhaust, shops and people, I could pick out her scent—earthy geranium and sharp clove. My belly tightened at the scent and my damn dick went stiff as a rod. I considered ditching the bike, shifting, and following her on paws then she swung through the gates of a townhouse development. I parked behind a nearby strip shopping center and prowled the fence until I found her scent again.

Going over the wall was easy. I paced

her, staying out of sight using the landscaping, parked cars, and a building. She lived at the very back of the place. I watched her key into one of the one-story units on the end of the building. Good. Time to wait.

🐾 🐾 🐾 🐾

Leigh

I SHUT THE DOOR and locked it—including the deadbolt. I didn't often do that until I went to bed but the hair on my neck had been standing on end since I walked out of the arson office. It was like someone had been watching. I tried to check people out, without being obvious, but never caught anyone who seemed all that interested. Weird. I normally didn't get all hinky like that. Of course, I'd been without sleep for over 24 hours and there was that whole "wreck my car then get rescued by the sexy biker" episode.

My palms itched with just the thought of him. Which walked right out of weird and slammed head-first into crazy. There was something so familiar about him and I'd swear on a stack of Bibles that I'd never seen him before, much less met him. He was sexy trouble and I didn't have time for any sort of distraction. If I was right, this morning's fire was just the latest in a string.

I stripped out of my clothes and stumbled into the bathroom. I wanted a hot shower and at least eight hours of sleep. And food. I hadn't had any more sustenance than I'd had sleep. Granted, coffee was its own food group, but it didn't exactly fill the tummy. I changed up my plans because I could be flexible. Shower, food, bed. Awesome.

As steaming water poured over my head, I thought about that morning's scene. The warehouse was located in a run-down area of southeast Dallas. I'd tracked down a couple of witnesses who complained about motorcycles and loud trucks coming and going in the past few days. And wasn't that interesting…since a guy on a bike just happened to show up and stuck to me like a cockle burr.

There'd been two other suspicious fires—one at a known drug house. The occupants had been driven out, then the place was torched. The second fire was in one of those self-storage places. Whatever was in the unit where the fire started had gone up like a roman candle. The place was a total loss, like the warehouse. I made mental note to call a cop buddy who was on DPD's gang unit.

The water was trickling lukewarm. Time to get out. Food. Bed. Yippee. I was more than ready. Hopefully, by letting my hamster wheel of a brain twirl in the shower, it would shut down and let me actually sleep. Drying off, I wrapped the towel around my wet hair and shrugged into my ratty old robe. It was fleece. And soft. I opened the bathroom door— and screamed!

FOUR

Smoke

MY EARS RANG from her scream and I leaned back just in time to miss the fist she aimed at my face. The bitch was fast—she followed up with a knee to my balls and I twisted just in time to block her with my hip.

"Yo, chill, Leigh." I held up my hands and backed away.

"What the hell are you doing here? How did you get in? Get out!"

I leaned up against the wall and watched. If she charged me again, I could wrap her up, keep her from hurting either of us. I didn't like the shadows under her eyes or how gaunt she looked. She needed sleep and food. As her tirade ran down, I turned and headed for the kitchen.

"C'mon. I'll feed you."

She sputtered into silence and stood there in the hallway, stiff and angry. I hoped she had something in the fridge I could throw together. I had the feeling that if I left to get food, she'd rabbit as soon as my back was turned. Rummaging in the fridge and freezer, I kept my focus on her. She darted to the front door, checked the locks. She huffed out a breath. There wasn't a lock in the world that could keep me away from her.

Leigh sidled into the kitchen and propped her prime ass on a tall kitchen stool. "What are you doing?"

"Feeding you." I'd found eggs, deli ham, mushrooms, shredded cheddar and a jar of jalapenos. I could work with this. I prepped. She stared holes in my back. When her frying pan was just hot enough, I poured in enough beaten eggs to coat the bottom.

"You're cooking."

"Yeah."

She scrubbed the heels of her hands against her face. "I'm dreaming. Or I fell in the shower and hit my head. Really hard."

She was too cute, if totally exhausted. "None of the above. Just because I ride a bike and wear a cut doesn't mean I can't take care of you."

"See, that's what I don't get. Why are you here?"

"I just told you. I'm here to take care of you."

"Yeah, like that's not creepy. And how the hell did you get in? I know I dead-bolted the door."

"It's keyed."

"What?" She blinked at me, bleary-eyed.

"Your dead bolt. It's keyed. Any lock that's keyed can be picked."

"You picked my locks?" Her voice was full of righteous outrage.

I didn't reply. I was busy turning the

omelet and adding the ham, cheese, mushrooms, and jalapenos. I plated her food, slid it onto the bar between her kitchen and living area. "Sit."

She sputtered at me. "I'm not some dog you can just—" Her nose twitched and she inhaled. "What is that?"

"What does it look like? Food, babe. An omelet."

She blinked several times in rapid succession. "You made me an omelet?"

"Yeah…" I turned back to the stove to make my own.

"*You* made an omelet."

I ignored the skepticism in her voice, but she climbed fully onto the barstool and forked a bite into her mouth. She made *mmm* noises. Good enough for me. I finished mine, plated it and ate standing up. Not bad.

Leigh didn't speak as she ate, and she didn't look up until her plate was empty. "You have a lot of explaining to do, buster."

"Yes, I picked your locks."

Her jaw dropped and when she realized her mouth was gaping, she snapped it shut. "That's breaking and entering."

"So arrest me."

"Don't think I won't. Why are you here?"

I didn't stop the instinctual smile. "I'm here for you, babe."

"Stop calling me that."

"Doesn't matter what I call you, you're still my babe."

She muttered under her breath. I caught

a few words—men, babe, ego, sexy, jerk. Yeah, I pretty much fit all those words. Except the babe part. I wondered if she knew how sexy she was when she got all serious and wore her official face. Did she carry handcuffs? Granted, she was an arson investigator, not a cop, but in my experience—and I had a hellava lot of it—Arson liked to make arrests as much as the next LEO. We could have a lot of fun with her handcuffs. I'd have to check the place out to see. If she didn't have any, maybe I'd bring my own.

Leigh inhaled, let it out slow. Her eyes were closed so she didn't catch me admiring the way her robe parted to reveal the sweet curve of her tits when she breathed like that. I was focused on her eyes when she opened them.

"Get out of my house."

"You need sleep." I had this insane desire to take care of her and she looked like shit. The shadows under her eyes made her look like some asshole had popped her in both eyes.

"What I I need is you out of my house."

"I'll leave as soon as you're asleep."

She threw up her arms. "*Argh!*"

Too cute. "Babe, go to bed. I'll clean up your kitchen and let myself out."

"Seriously? How stupid do you think I am?"

I studied her, focused entirely on her face. "I don't think you're stupid at all, Leigh. I do think that you've hit the end of your body's ability to function. Go to bed. I'll be gone when you wake up."

I came around the bar, grabbed the lapels of her robe and pulled. She slid off the stool and her knees wobbled. I scooped her up, carried her down the hall to her bedroom. I'd already checked it out while she was in the shower, just like I had her entire condo. She didn't bring any paperwork home with her. I hadn't had a chance to crack her laptop. I would, but not today.

Tucking her into bed, I backed away. "Sleep, babe. I promise. I'll clean your kitchen then boogie."

"Why…" A huge yawn interrupted her. "…should I trust you?"

"You shouldn't," I teased as I started to shut her door. "But you will." I didn't close the door all the way. And I made sure to make noise walking down the hallway to the living area. For now, I'd play my game her way.

🐾🐾🐾🐾

Leigh

"TRUST ME, HE SAYS." Yeah, right. I trusted him as far as I could throw him. Considering he was about 6'3" and 220 pounds, I couldn't even pick him up. Drag him, sure. Pick up and throw? Not a snowball's chance. My kitchen was spotless and Smoke was nowhere to be found. I trudged to the front door to make sure it was locked.

Leaning against the door, I pulled the towel off my head and scrubbed at my hair. It was damp and would frizz but I was exhausted. That was my story and I'd stick to it. Why else would I have let an armed and dangerous man into my house without calling 9-1-1? Forget that he was sexy and steamrolled right over me. Ugh. I thumped my head against the door—and heard a deep, rumbling chuckle. What the—?

I whirled, jerked open the door and glared. But Smoke was twenty feet away, straddling his Harley, looking all smug. That was it. I'd officially been awake long enough to have aural hallucinations.

"Get some sleep, Leigh."

"Go away, Smoke."

"You sure that's what you want me to do, darlin'?"

"Positive." I was. Totally. The idea of curling up next to his hard body didn't appeal at all. Not one tiny bit. Nuh-uh. Nope. He laughed and I realized I just let out a gusty and deeply feminine sigh of…something. Not desire. I didn't even like this guy. Even if he could make a mean omelet. And had shaggy dark hair I wanted to comb my fingers through.

I blinked, realizing I'd been staring blankly. Yup, that smirk was still plastered on his face. I bet he'd ride off and go nail some helpless bimbo.

"Sorry to disappoint you, babe, but

you're the only female I intend to nail any time in the near future. But I want you well-rested and fully awake when I do. Now go inside, lock the door, and sleep. I have to get to work."

Work? The guy worked? My brain was so fuzzy I wasn't quite comprehending. Did bikers actually have jobs? Like they got up, punched a time clock, and worked forty-hour weeks? I mean, this guy was an outlaw biker. I might not be up on all the gang stuff but even I recognized that 1% patch he wore.

"Babe."

I blinked again. And discovered my vision was graying a bit at the edges. The next thing I knew, I'd been scooped up into Smoke's arms and he was carrying me inside. Some inner feminine creature that had nothing to do with me plastered my nose against his neck and we—what was surely a demon succubus and I—inhaled deeply. He smelled of leather and wind and just a hint of cherry, like expensive pipe tobacco...

I OPENED MY EYES to darkness, my heart hammering, and my chest tight from holding my breath. I listened hard. Nothing. I didn't remember getting into bed. I remembered...being in Smoke's arms and breathing him in. Crud. I was alone in bed and a mental "service check" let me know that no hanky or panky had occurred while I'd been passed out.

Snagging my cell phone from the table beside my bed, I checked the time. 12:02. My curtains were shut tight. My cyes wcrc still a little blurry so I looked at my phone again. AM. Wow. I'd been asleep for almost twelve hours. And now my sleep schedule was all messed up. I needed to go back to sleep because I had regular duty in the morning, reporting at 7 AM. Yippee.

A yawn and a big stretch didn't help. Then my stomach grumbled. I'd missed dinner. And lunch. Though that omelet Smoke fixed me sort of counted as brunch. But I was hungry. Not quite *hangry* yet but I would be soon. I shuffled out of bed and froze. I'd been wearing a robe. Now I wore a tank and a loose-fitting pair of gym shorts.

When had I changed? *Had* I changed? Smoke. That...jerk. *Now* I was hangry and I marched into the kitchen. I was up and there'd be no going back to sleep. How dare he!?! The work light over my stove was on and there was a bag with a note propped up against it.

Robes aren't for sleeping. I took the liberty. Liked what I saw. I'll be seeing more of it. Eat. Later, babe. ~S

I wadded up the note and flung it toward the trashcan. I missed by a mile. I glared at the sack. It carried the logo of my favorite sub shop. Inside, I found a giant sub with meat. And another note. **Veggies and dressing in fridge. Eat it all. You'll need to keep up your strength. ~S**

Oh! The freaking arrogance of this man! He broke into my house not once but twice. And he was feeding me. What was that all about? My stomach snarled. Loudly. Fine. I'd eat. I dug in my fridge for the take-out containers. Shredded lettuce. Onions. Jalapeños. And oil and vinegar. How did he know what I ate?

My stomach growled, its message clear. "Yo! Food. Now, woman!"

Fine. I'd eat the food he left me. Then I'd figure out a lock he couldn't pick.

FIVE

Leigh

MY ALARM WENT OFF at 5:30 AM. My eyes didn't want to open and my brain was groggy. Unable to decide if I'd had too much sleep or not enough, I stumbled into the bathroom to start the morning necessities—pee, brushing teeth, then coffee. I managed the first two then dragged down the hallway to my kitchen. Normally, I set up the coffeemaker the night before. I'd forgotten but as I turned the corner, my nose was filled with the thick, rich scent of fresh dark roast coffee.

I freaked out. Just a little. There were no notes. No box of donuts. My front door was secure. Maybe I'd forgotten and programmed the darn thing after all. I managed to pour a cup without spilling and added a spoonful of sugar. With mug in hand, I wandered back to my bedroom—and realized there was something wrong with the left side of the bed. I sleep on the right—closest to the bathroom door. The left-side pillow was bunched up but with a distinct impression in the middle. The covers on that side of the bed were all wonky too. What the hell? I scrubbed at my face, forgetting I had a mug of hot coffee in my hand. *Ow!*

This was not going to be a good day.

Walking through the door exactly one minute before my shift started, I headed directly to the break room for coffee. I'd managed to clean up my mess, throw coffee-stained clothes and towels in the washer, grab a shower and make it on time. But I was functioning on half a cup of coffee.

I spent the day pretty much chained to my desk doing file searches and researching databases for clues about the identity of my arsonist. My new FD sedan arrived, and I got to drive it home instead of taking the bus. Lost in thought while stopped at a stoplight, I heard a motorcycle rev beside me and I jumped. I turned to glare, figuring it would be that obnoxious Smoke but it wasn't. The guy was staring at me and it creeped me out. Still, I glared at him and arched a brow in that universal facial expression of "You want some of this? You ain't got what it takes, sucker."

He rode off as soon as the light turned green and I realized the emblem on the back of his leather jacket was different. He wore an ugly-ass dog thing with horns. Hell Dogs MC. Yeah, I definitely needed to check with my buddy in the DPD gang unit. He had to know something about outlaw bikers.

Though the biker was long gone, I still had the feeling of being watched. All the way home. I parked and sat in the car for a few minutes. Not sure what I was waiting for, I just didn't feel comfortable getting out in the open—not even for the short walk to my front door. The feeling passed but I sat another couple of minutes. When it didn't come back, I jumped out and all but ran to my door.

I unlocked it but almost busted my nose when I tried to open it and walk in at the same time. What the hell? Then I remembered that I'd double locked the door. I had to search for the key to the deadbolt and I was fumbling by the time I found it, got it inserted, and turned. The hair on my neck was prickling something fierce. Before I closed the door behind me, I scanned the parking lot. Nothing appeared to be out of place. No strange cars or people— just a big, shaggy German Shepherd mix lying on the grass of the green belt across the way.

Beer and food—in that order. That's what I wanted. I stripped off my uniform shirt and kicked off my boots. Then I grabbed a beer and riffled through the freezer for a frozen dinner. Picking one at random, I tossed it in the microwave, opened my beer, and settled on the couch to watch the news.

The arsons weren't the lead story— thank goodness—but they were covered. The microwave dinged and I ate stoically. I needed to find time to shop for groceries. And I needed to get over being a weenie. I was an arson investigator. I did dangerous things. Running out at night to grab fast food was not a dangerous thing. But the idea of walking out into the dark almost froze me in place.

Fine. I had other stuff to do anyway. Important stuff. Like laundry. Cleaning the toilets. I'd get right on all that as soon as I caught up on my DVR'd episodes of NCIS.

❧

I WOKE UP IN BED. Wearing sleep shorts and a tank. I didn't remember going to bed. This was just crazy. I rolled over and stared at my cell phone. 5:55 AM. Wide awake, I rushed through my morning routine. There was no tell-tale sign that anyone had been in my house. No notes. No coffee set to brew— which sort of bummed me out...

There was no way I could be having blackouts. I'd just had my yearly departmental physical and I was in perfect health. Maybe I really was just that tired. Or I was sleepwalking. Except it was cold at night. I normally wore flannel sleep pants and a T-shirt. Not...shorts and a tank. Yeah...not cool.

I didn't want to consider the other possibility. I'd almost rather have a brain tumor given the alternative—that Smoke had broken in *again*, found me asleep on the couch and put me to bed.

Time to turn the tables. I'd give my DPD buddy a call and I'd go track down Smoke's sorry ass and confront him. I inhaled deeply and things settled inside me. That was the ticket. I'd stalk him for a change. I was totally on board for that.

After a few phone calls and a pinky swear that I wouldn't do anything without police backup, I parked my rather blatant, if nondescript, sedan half a block away from the Nightriders' Dallas compound not far from Love Field. About twenty bikes were parked in front of a one-story cement-block building. A twelve-foot high chain-link fence wrapped around the compound. The place had been a wrecker yard in a previous lifetime. Evidently, the Nightriders took it over, running Rider Tow and Salvage. I could see cars parked behind the building and two two trucks, a roll-back wrecker, and a huge sucker used for semi-trucks were lined up along the side.

I couldn't tell one motorcycle from the next, but I watched the bikers come and go throughout the afternoon. At one point, two of them stood next to the gate staring up the street at me. I slouched down, noting the sun was bouncing off the windshield and they shouldn't be able to see me. Still, it was disconcerting. I needed to move along before they got truly suspicious and came to check the car.

As soon as the coast was clear, I started the sedan and headed back to my office. I had more research to do, then I was going home and drinking coffee until I floated. No way was I going to sleep tonight. Not until I solved the mystery of how I kept ending up in bed.

By the time I got home, my eyes were bleary from reading files and staring at my computer monitor. I started a pot of coffee and grabbed another microwave meal. I desperately needed to make time to hit the grocery store. I didn't cook much but that didn't mean I was incapable of fixing real food. It just seemed such a waste to cook for one. Still, the microwave stuff was getting old.

The day had been unseasonable warm so I stripped down to the tank top I wore under my uniform shirt, kicked off my boots and got comfortable. As the minutes ticked by, I sipped coffee and read through a file I'd grabbed on my way out—a list of serial arsonists and their MO my predecessor had put together before he retired. One file niggled at the back of my brain—an arsonist tagged *The Ghost*. No one knew who this guy was but he was a professional. I rolled my eyes at the nickname. I kept reading, fascinated despite myself. He had a signature trigger—one that resembled some found by the military in IEDs. He was like the Robin Hood of people had given him.

The timer dinged and I set a mental alarm for two minutes—the time the instructions said to let it sit before eating. I continued to read the information on this Ghost dude. A shiver finger-walked up my spine, accompanied by that creepy feeling people described as "someone just walked the hell over my grave."

Smoke. Smoke was like fog, which was spooky and all ghostly and stuff. I tried to shake off the feeling. Yes, indeedy. I was totally unnerved now but things were starting to click. Had Smoke been stalking me? From the very beginning? I mean, what were the odds that he'd be on that road at that time of the morning just in time to rescue me?

"You're thinking too hard, babe."

🐾 🐾 🐾 🐾

Smoke

I WINCED as Leigh screamed. I admit, I was a bit surprised that she was such a girly-girl about stuff like this. Then again, she was too cute when she did it so I wasn't going to complain.

"Where did you come from!"

"The front door."

"Breaking and entering!"

"Entering, yeah. I'll give you that, but I didn't break anything."

She scowled at me and fisted her hands on her hips and thrusting out her chest, which made her tits do some very interesting things in that tank top.

"You are nothing more than a scary-ass stalker."

I couldn't stop the slow grin spreading across my face even if I wanted to. "Definitely scary-ass. Stalker? Babe, I'm just getting started."

Leigh gulped and I watched her throat work. My dick perked right up, wondering how far she could swallow it. My brain—and dick—was focused on that and would be until I got between her legs.

"Do you realize how creepy that sounds?" She nodded like one of those bobble-head things. "Yup. Totally creepy. Go away. And stop breaking into my house."

"You need to eat."

She threw up her hands, which revealed skin above her belt buckle. Yeah, totally kissing my way from that spot until I got all the way to heaven.

"What is it about you and feeding me?"

"It just is. You're too skinny."

She sputtered, her mouth opened. Closed. She sputtered some more. "Too skinny?"

I nodded. I'm a big man. I like some soft on my women. She was hot standing there with not much on but I wouldn't bitch if she added a few pounds.

Leigh remained shocked. What was the word? Aghast. Yeah. That's how she looked. "Haven't you heard that saying? A girl can't be too rich or too skinny?"

"Yeah she can."

"You are totally weird, Smoke."

"Nope. Just a man who loves women and doesn't care how much money they have."

Her eyes narrowed and her lips formed an "O" that made my dick throb. "So..." She drew out the syllable. "You're one of those guys."

"Yeah. So?"

"So, a smart woman wouldn't do you at all. A desperate woman would need a full body condom. Just FYI? I'm not desperate."

Too fucking cute.

She tilted her head and studied me, then jutted her chin in my direction. "I don't like you."

"And?"

"Are you in the habit of screwing women you don't like?"

"I refer you to my previous statement. I'm a man who loves women." Except the more time I spent around Leigh, the less appealing every other woman became.

"And you have too been stalking me."

🐾 🐾 🐾 🐾

Leigh

I STOOD STILL, despite the on-going argument with my lizard brain which insisted I was in danger, that I was...prey. I almost agreed as he prowled toward me. His eyes burned with an intensity I found disconcerting and that smile curling his lips up at the corners was as lethal as any weapon pointed at my heart.

"Babe," he chided. "We've been stalking each other for a couple of days."

"Speak for yourself."

"You think we didn't see you at the clubhouse?" He laughed, this big, virile man who called himself Smoke. He was Mr. Biker Badass, and my inner cavewoman wanted him like damn and whoa. I slapped the bitch down—or tried. He stretched his hand toward me, cupped my cheek before I managed to muzzle her.

"You know this is going to happen." His deep, growling voice touched my skin. I could literally feel the words brushing against me. Then he bent, grazed my lips with his, and everything female sighed, then promptly melted into a big ol' pile of girly-goo.

This was wrong, on so many levels, but what the hell. Common sense was gone, carried out on a wave of cheerleading girly bits. I wanted him. Needed him. He was Compulsion with a capital C, all dressed up and ready for a Girl's Night Out at the Magic Mike review.

"This is a bad idea." I managed to murmur the words against his mouth.

"Babe."

I melted. Again. From the inside out. He was a bad idea masquerading as a good one, and I knew I would give in to the sheer maleness of him. I had no choice.

"Kiss me."

I wanted to.

He cupped my face with one hand and then his mouth was on mine, teasing, almost like he was testing to see what I tasted like. He was so gentle I opened almost out of instinct. The fingers of his other hand danced like lightning over my bare skin. His tongue swept through my mouth. I gripped his shoulders, bracing against them because I was suddenly on tiptoes. He was all male, lean muscle flexing beneath tan skin. I couldn't get enough of him.

He took over, fisting my ponytail, controlling me, pulling my head back so he could deepen the kiss. My knees locked and I swayed. I could lean forward, press against him, find my balance, but I didn't. Something stopped me. His lips brushed along my neck, his breath feathering across my pulse point one of the most erotic things I'd ever experienced. And he hadn't even gotten me naked yet.

What was it about this man? I was a smart woman. Grounded. Self-confident. But one look from him and my common sense ran for the hills. I wanted to tear my clothes off. Tear his off. I didn't do things like this. I was careful. Guarded.

His thumb feathered over my nipple and I couldn't breathe. Even through my tank and sports bra, his touch branded me. I couldn't remember every being kissed in a way that made me feel...what? Like Smoke wanted to devour me? Like he had no place else to be, nothing else to do but kiss me? Like I was the only woman in the world. Heady stuff, that feeling.

A kiss, I reminded myself. Just a kiss. We'd known each other a matter of days. This connection shouldn't exist. But it did. My heart knew it. And my head.

"I can't get enough of you, baby," he murmured against my breast. Then his lips found mine and proved to me how hungry he was. Breathless, he rested his forehead against mine. Every muscle in my body was tense and I was still on tiptoes. I started to shake.

"Trying to be good here," I murmured. Trying to be sane was more like it.

That's when his big hands wrapped around my ribs and lifted me. My legs automatically circled his waist and I almost moaned. He had a major boner going behind the buttons of those Levis.

"You're good, babe. Trust me." And he let loose that wicked laugh that went straight to my womb and made me quiver all over.

"Touch me," I ordered, pulling my tank over my head.

"You don't have to ask twice," he agreed as I jerked at his jacket. It was gone in an instant, his black tee shirt following a blink later.

He didn't give me a chance to lose my bra. He ripped it in half, right down the middle. Holy hell, the man had some strong hands.

"Fuck. You're too good to be true. Gotta be dreamin' this." He buried his face between my breasts.

Somebody moaned. I think it was me. I leaned back as he sucked one of my nipples into his mouth. Too good. This felt too good. Too fast. I rolled my hips, rubbing my clit against his cock. I didn't even get embarrassed at how wet I was.

"Want more, babe?"

How could he sound so...normal? So

calm. Hell yeah I wanted more. I wanted it all. "Yes." I moaned the word.

He grinned and dear Lord, I was ready to beg. "Good. I'm going to make you come now."

Yes! I wanted to throw confetti. Toast with champagne. But then we were in my bedroom and he was laying me down on the bed. He followed me down, covering me, his weight settling between my thighs. I whimpered, ready to beg.

Smoke hooked an arm under my knee, hitched it up and pressed his body against mine. He rubbed his cock, hiding behind those brass buttons, against my clit. It should have hurt, would have if I'd been naked. Then suddenly I was. My duty pants were gone, my plain cotton panties shredded and those big brass buttons were right there pressing, rubbing, circling. Too much. Too much sensation. It hurt but the pain was exquisite.

He kissed me as he rolled his hips, his tongue deep in my mouth, demanding I respond. His hand cupped my ass, held me still while he worked me.

"You like this."

It wasn't a question, but I answered him anyway. "God yes!"

He bit my bottom lip. Hard. I tasted blood and didn't care. His lips moved as restlessly as his hips. Nipping my earlobe, my shoulder, my breast. His hips twisted and I went blind as shooting stars filled my vision.

Something hard speared me roughly and

I fought. Finger. He'd pushed his finger into me. Two fingers. Three. Rough, calloused, long. He worked me. In and out as I convulsed around him, the aftereffects of my orgasm still rocking my body. I rode his hand, climbing fast and a second orgasm, just as amazing as the first, burst through me.

I hooked the back of his neck, kissed him, open-mouthed and demanding. He jerked away from me, stared down at my face then his eyes switched focus.

"Gonna fuck that mouth," he growled, and I climaxed again. Then his cock was inside me and I couldn't remember anything else.

SIX

Leigh

I WOKE UP HOT, sweaty, and pinned in bed. Adrenaline surged, which made me hotter and sweatier. I breathed through the initial panic. I was in my bed, after all. Focusing my caffeine-deprived brain took some doing. Okay, so my state of mind wasn't entirely due to lack of caffeine. I had been thoroughly fucked. Several times. If I remembered correctly. At the moment, the man who'd left me in this state was sleeping soundly on his stomach, face turned away, but one muscular arm draped across my stomach. I tucked my chin so I could get a better look at him.

Ink. He had ink. I didn't like tattoos, had been raised to think them low-class but his… Oh my God, his back was a work of art. The patch on his leather vest had been perfectly recreated but with a lot of artistic license. The leaping wolf wasn't stylized. He was perfectly formed and shaded in silver and black, the ears rimmed in brown. The leaping front feet were silvery-white, and the body trailed off into a comet tail of red-hot colors.

"Like what you see?"

I'd been staring at his back so intently, I

didn't realize he'd turned his head to face me. My fingers itched to trace the wolf—to pet it...him.

"I don't like tattoos."

Smoke gave me a sloe-eyed blink and smiled. "Uh huh." He rolled to his side, shifting me with him. "Funny. My tattoo likes you."

He cupped my breast and I swallowed the gasp his touch caused. I pushed at his chest and pretended my fingers didn't brush through the feathering of dark hair highlighting his pecs.

"I might not be in the mood."

"Oh?" He trailed a finger over my ribs—light and teasing but I'm not ticklish. "I guess you'll just have to lay here and take it. This won't take long."

His hand pulled my calf up over his hip then his fingers brushed between my thighs, getting intimate fast. I was already wet. He smiled and winked.

"Not long at all."

I feigned a yawn. "Good. I have other things to—"

His fingers pushed into me and I couldn't speak, couldn't breathe. Nope. Wasn't going to take long at all. My insides were already churning and the muscles in my vagina were pulsing as they tightened around his intrusion.

🐾

Smoke

"GREEDY LITTLE THING," I murmured against her ear. I could feel her heartbeat in her pussy. I curled two fingers against her G-spot, and she moaned. When I pressed my thumb against her clit, her hands spasmed, driving her nails into my skin.

Her eyes flew open when she realized she'd drawn blood. She looked panicked as she apologized. "Sorry!"

I smirked while my wolf preened just beneath my skin. He liked that our mate bloodied us. There wasn't another woman in the world, he reminded me, who could arouse and challenge us like this one did. I kissed her, claiming her mouth. I worked her pussy with my hand until she was squirming against me. "Did I mention this won't take long?"

Leigh uttered a startled laugh when I closed my teeth over her nipple. I nipped, licked, nipped again, and sucked hard.

"Well alrighty then." Her voice was rough and husky with need. "I guess I have a few minutes."

"I 'preciate you makin' the time, babe." I rolled her to her back and kissed my way down to the thatch of silky hair at the junction of her thighs. I sat up, grabbed her knees and spread her. "Beautiful pussy." It was, all pink and wet and waiting for me to taste. I settled between her legs.

I heard her breath catch when I licked

between her folds. Her muscles twitched when I flicked the tip of my tongue over her clit, but it was the gasping moan when I thrust my tongue into her channel that got me so hard I thought I might shoot my wad right then. I pushed into the heat and away again, teasing—or tormenting if her protests were to be believed. Her pulse thundered against my tongue.

Her thighs pressed against my shoulders and her hips danced beneath me. I had to use a forearm across her belly to keep her still so I could continue to eat her out. Damn but she tasted good. I'd never stop hungering for her. She pushed against me, feet on the bed now so she could arch higher as a scream broke from between her lips and she melted beneath, panting and quivering as I pushed three fingers in as I used my mouth on her clit.

"Again," I ordered, pushing her to the quivering edge a second time. "Again, babe."

She shook her head, hair tangled across the pillow and she fought. Her hands loosened their grip on the sheets and found my hair. She tugged and jerked, trying to force my mouth away from her cunt. Wasn't happening. She screamed this time and I could all but see her fly off into space. Her breaths came in little wheezing sobs as I sat up and rolled away. "My work here is done."

"The hell you say!" She snarled at me and as quick as a snake, she had me pushed down on the bed. I admit I let her because I was curious. Would she suck me off or would she ride me?

Stretching out, I tucked my hands behind my head and watched her.

"Whatcha' gonna do, babe?"

"This," she hissed, straddling me. My dick was as hard as granite and precum leaked from its tip. She rubbed her wet pussy up the length of my dick as she leaned forward. Planting her hands on either side of my head, she stared at my mouth.

"Kiss me," I ordered. I wanted her to taste herself on me. When she resisted, I fisted one hand in her hair and pressed her head down. I took her mouth, feasted on it just like I had her pussy. Damn but I loved the taste of her. Would never be satisfied. I broke the kiss.

Leigh rested her forehead against mine, panting. "You have two choices, babe. Fuck me or suck me."

Her head jerked up and she glared. "You're *so* romantic."

Sarcasm. I liked it. My dick twitched against her, reminding her of what was waiting for her. "You think?"

She wormed her way down my body and settled on her knees between my thighs. Staring at my dick, she licked her lips. I groaned and she smiled. Dipping down, she flicked her tongue over the head of my dick, and it twitched against her lips. She grabbed it with one hand and treated it like an ice cream cone. Oh, hell yeah. The way her lips and tongue glided over me? She could spend hours...fuck, she could spend days sucking me off. Her mouth was gawddamned magic.

She worked me—mouth and hands—and it was all I could do not to grab her head, hold her still, and fuck her mouth. Would she swallow when I came? That wasn't a question with the sweet butts who hung around the clubhouse. They swallowed or else. But this was Leigh. I was keeping her. We'd negotiate the finer points when my dick wasn't throbbing

I froze. My brain finally caught up with the rest of me and my wolf. Keeping her? Mate? What the fuck? I sucked in a breath. The damn gods were fuckin' with me. The arsonist and the arson investigator. We were a fucking match made in hell.

Leigh moaned around my dick and her hand went between her legs. Fuckin' A. She was getting turned on by suckin' me off. Maybe the gods weren't so crazy after all. I pulled out of her mouth and she made a little mewling sound in protest. Gripping her biceps, I lifted her and set her down straddling me.

"Ride me, Leigh."

She wrapped her fingers around me and pressed the head of my dick against her opening. She was so freaking hot and slick that I slid right in and she took me. All of me. She stared at me for about thirty seconds and then she started to move.

Holy. Hell.

When I came, I thought I'd blown the top off my dick. My cum pumped into her as I shuddered beneath her. She was leaning, her hands braced on my chest, her whole body quivering. I wasn't sure either of us was breathing. I wasn't capable of it in that moment. I managed two words.

"Fuck, babe."

Leigh sucked in air, expanding her chest. Her tits were right there so I cupped them, causing her breath to quicken. Her skin was sheened with perspiration and heat radiated from her. Laughing, she climbed off me and flopped onto her back. She smirked at me but managed to look prim at the same time.

"*That* ought to do it."

She looked so damn proud. Too fucking cute for words.

Leigh

I'M NOT A RELIGIOUS person but if that wasn't Nirvana, there was no such thing. No man should be hung that well, have that kind of staying power, and taste so good. I've never been a BJ kinda gal, but Smoke could have me rethinking that in a heartbeat.

Lying there catching my breath, I pretended to be all cocky and self-assured like I had mind-blowing sex every day. Yeah. Right. I wasn't a virgin. I'd had several guys in my life and enjoyed the sexy times. But Smoke? He took sex to a whole other level. This was a man who knew what made a woman tick. Boy did he! I remembered to inhale and heard him chuckle.

"You ready for round..." He held up his hand and started counting on his fingers. Not fair. I'd lost count of the climaxes he'd given me.

"No. We're done. I have work."

"No. We aren't done and today is Saturday. You aren't on the duty roster."

How did he know that? "How do you know?"

"I called and asked. You aren't even on call."

He rolled over on top of me, pushing his hips between my thighs. His cock was still hard! How was that even possible? I winced as it rubbed against my hyper-sensitized clit. He immediately raised his hips, breaking contact.

"Shit, babe. I didn't stop to think. Are you sore?"

Come to think of it, I was a tad tender down there. Before I could respond, he was up and padding to the bathroom. Poets would write sonnets in praise of his ass. Me? I just wanted to hug it and pet it and call it George. I might even throw in some kisses. He returned with a warm washcloth and very tenderly cleaned me. Though slightly embarrassed, it was still quite erotic yet sweet as all get out. I was done for. This guy was all wrong for me, but I had no choice in the matter. I'd fallen and fallen hard. And I'd be praying to the God I wasn't sure existed in that I wasn't making a horrible mistake.

SEVEN

Smoke

THE LAST THING I needed was to get swept up in the mating heat. There's a reason Wolves say we're "moonstruck" when we find our mate. I didn't have time for all that bullshit. The Russian expected me to do my job and no one disappointed the Russian—well, no one had survived who did. Since I didn't have a death wish, I needed to get my job done. Then I could figure out what the hell to do with Leigh—besides fucking us both blind every chance I got.

By Sunday, I'd moved in with her—which meant I grabbed my saddlebags from a spare room at the Dallas chapter's clubhouse and draped it over a chair in Leigh's bedroom. But now it was Friday and time to get on with my job. The Dallas chapter had a bunch of human hang-arounds, far more than any other chapter. I wasn't too sure about them. Same went for the chapter president, Boner. Hardy, our national VP, wanted to know if they passed the sniff test. They didn't. The Russian and our national board would have to deal with Boner sooner or later.

Boner was a bastard and there was

history—bad history. I didn't know the whole story but why the man was still president was beyond me. He was the one pulling in the human hang-arounds and wanting to make them prospects. The rank and file Wolves were none too happy about that situation. I'd picked up grumbles before I met Leigh.

As much as I wanted to spend all my time with her, I couldn't. Some nights, I didn't get back until she was sound asleep. Some nights I got home and she was gone—called out to a fire scene to investigate. So far, there'd been no more suspicious fires that concerned me. That wouldn't last.

We'd been together just over two weeks and she hadn't questioned my absences. Yet. I couldn't decide if she didn't care or was too nervous to ask. I caught occasional wafts of scalded milk which indicated she was a little nervous. Hell, I was as nervous as a coon walking past a pack of hounds. The irony of the two of us being mates was something that smacked me in the face every time she got a call out.

I rolled up to the space assigned to her and parked in front of her SUV. She had two spaces with her condo. Leigh had been nice enough to back the Highlander out a little so I could leave my bike in front of it. Her POS FD sedan squatted in the second slot. I opened the front door and paused. Leigh was in the living area and the stench of burnt toast filled my nose. She glanced my direction then ignored me.

I watched her. Back and forth. Back and forth, her gait not quite a march. The odor didn't dissipate. She was totally pissed. I folded my arms across my chest, leaned a shoulder against the door jamb and waited for her anger to cool. When it didn't, I jumped in. "Ah, Leigh?"

"What!"

Okay. That was a snarling demand, not a question. I was feeling brave so, in a low-pitched voice, I asked, "Wanna tell me why you're pissed?"

"No!"

"Wanna stop pacing?"

"I can't stop!"

Well, okay then. "Why not?"

"I'm too pissed."

"Uh-huh." Back to square one. "Wanna tell me why?"

"No!"

"Babe."

"Stop that."

"Babe."

Leigh threw her hands in the air as she stopped right in front of me. "My sister."

Yeah, family could make even the best of us nuts. "Okay. Wanna tell me about your sister?"

"Oh hell no!"

"Babe."

"*ARGH!*"

A moment later, she stopped in front of me. Leaning forward, she bumped her forehead against my chest. I settled my arms around her and walked her backwards so I could close the door. I kicked it shut and kept walking her toward the couch. Now that she was relaxing, I'd get the whole story. I didn't have to wait long.

"She wants me to meet her for dinner tonight," she said to my chest.

That explained nothing. I made a noncommittal *uh-huh* sound.

"Her and her fiancé."

"Uh huh."

"He's...he's..." She pushed off my chest, shrugged out of my hug, and started pacing again.

"An asshole?"

"Yes. A handsome, rich, obnoxious asshole."

"Uh huh."

"Shut up, Smoke. You do the same thing with that word as you do with—"

"Babe." Laughing, I dodged as a heavy glass bowl sailed at my head. I snatched it out of the air and set it out of her reach. "I don't see the problem."

"That's because you're a man. Lindsay is my younger sister. She's beautiful. Talented. And she's engaged to one of the most eligible men in Dallas."

"Still not seein' the problem, babe. You're beautiful. Intelligent. And you've got me."

"You are *not* Justin. Wait...you think I'm beautiful?"

"Babe." I grabbed her before she could

walk away and held her against my chest. "Yes. You're gorgeous but it isn't just your hot body that has me hard." I snagged her hand and pressed it against my dick. Damn that felt fucking amazing. "Maybe you should think about staying home instead."

She sighed softly and melted. "I wish. She wants to talk about her wedding. I'm maid of honor."

"Where and when?"

"Huh?"

"Dinner. Where and when, babe? I'll go with you."

"Oh...no, no, no."

I quirked an eyebrow. "You embarrassed to be seen with me?" I tried levity to keep from snarling.

She rocked back. I think I caught her off guard. "You'd actually go?"

"Sure."

An evil grin spread across her face. "Dressed like—" She waved her hands in my direction.

I looked down. Leather biker boots. Black jeans. Black tee shirt. My cut. "Uh...yeah." It's not like I even owned a suit and tie.

"Awesome!" She danced around the room, fist pumping. Then she returned to stand in front of me, cupped my face and laid a kiss on me. "Lindsay will be totally scandalized."

Shit. I'd just been played. I smiled. Evilly. Payback would be hell.

🐾 🐾 🐾 🐾

Leigh

I DIDN'T HATE my sister. In fact, I loved her. I just didn't *like* her very much. Lindsay was two years younger and her life had been charmed from the moment she cried the first time. My older brother had that same luck. He failed at nothing. Me? I'm the middle child and I packed all the middle-child baggage I could carry.

Standing outside of Bellamy's, the five-star restaurant, with Smoke, I almost turned tail and ran. What seemed like an amazing idea two hours ago now felt like it was going to reach up and bite me in the ass. I'd forgotten how hoity-toity this place was and I felt bad for Smoke. He didn't deserve this.

His palm rested warm and comforting against the small of my back. I glanced up and he didn't seem concerned at all. I ground my teeth as the maître d' approached, a disapproving frown on his face.

"Do you have reservations?" he asked, his tone sharp and snippy.

"We're meeting a party here...Dr. Justin White?"

The man sniffed, obviously finding us unworthy, despite my very respectable little black dress. He glanced at Smoke, his brows scrunched together, lips pursed. I watched his eyes widen and an emotion that looked a lot like fear flashed across his expression.

"Y-yes. Of course. Right this way please."

If the man had been a dog, his tail would be between his legs. I seriously thought he might crumple to the floor and go belly up. I glanced sharply at Smoke, but he looked like he always looked—cocky and slightly amused by the world around him. I spotted Lindsay and Justin occupying a prime table overlooking the enclosed gardens half a story below the wall of windows at the back of the restaurant. My sister was cooing at her fiancé and I rolled my eyes. Justin saw me first and his eyes squinted with disdain. Then he got a look at Smoke. I almost laughed.

We cut quite a swath through the place. The women were all but drooling. The men? Now their reactions were interesting—and revealing. I was a trained investigator. I knew all about body language, physical cues, et cetera. But the men? Half of them looked like they wanted to piss themselves and the other half looked like they wanted to kill Smoke on the spot. Justin stared daggers so I put him in the kill column.

Lindsay finally realized that she'd lost Justin's attention. I knew the moment she recognized the situation. I'd been prepared so my expression didn't change. Justin rose and with his feet planted shoulder-width apart, awaited our arrival at the table. The maître d' scurried off, leaving me to pull out my chair. My hand landed on the back of it to do just that when Smoke's hand covered mine. Without a word, he held the chair, helped scoot it closer to the table, all the while staring at Justin. I could almost smell the testosterone.

"Who's this?" Lindsay demanded, her voice shading to the shrill side.

"Smoke Jenner," he said, beating me to it—a good thing since I didn't even know his last name. How crazy was that? The guy was practically living with me and I'd never bothered to ask his last name. "You must be Lindsay."

I had to bite my lips. Smoke sounded perfectly nice but there was just enough intonation to imply she was somehow...inferior.

"Dr. Justin White." The jerk made no attempt to shake hands.

"Huh." Smoke sat beside me with no further comment. Talk about dismissing someone! Was I a terrible sister for hoping Smoke would still be in my life when the wedding rolled around? Of course, if he was, Lindsay might disown me, and I'd be off the hook. Yippee. I hated weddings. I especially hated society weddings.

Dinner went downhill from there. Justin ordered a pretentiously expensive bottle of wine and went through the whole wine sniffing and testing routine with the sommelier. I noticed the look Smoke exchanged with the man and after Justin pronounced the wine perfect, Smoke ordered a second bottle of something else.

Justin glowered while Smoke said to put it on a separate tab. With a knowing smile, the sommelier poured Justin's wine into our glasses then hurried off. I'd just taken my first swallow and had to work hard to keep from making a "bitter beer face" when the man was back with the second bottle. He uncorked it and started the entire process over.

"I just need the cork please," Smoke said. The man handed it to him and Smoke sniffed. "I'll pour, thank you." Wow, look at him being all polite. I was a tad shocked. He took the bottle from the sommelier as a busboy arrived with fresh wine glasses. Smoke poured wine into my glass and smiled. "This will suit your palate better, babe."

I wasn't a big wine drinker to begin with and if that stuff I'd just swallowed was any indication, I wasn't missing much. I took a hesitant sip. It tasted like sunshine and running barefoot in green grass. I wasn't sure my eyes didn't roll back in my head as the flavor burst on my tongue.

Smoke laughed and shared another long look with the sommelier. "I think she likes it."

"Not surprising, sir. You have excellent tastes."

Of course he did, my big, bad, scary biker. Sadly, as good as the wine and food tasted, the evening was a disaster. Justin acted like a total dick. Oh wait. He *was* a total dick. Lindsay acted like the spoiled princess, and I realized those two deserved each other.

I happily basked in the sexy glow that was all things Smoke.

During a long silence, Lindsay studied Smoke. "So, tell me, Smoke. What do you do for a living?"

I tensed and sat up straighter but before I could say anything, Smoke wrapped his hand around mine under the table and gave it a gentle squeeze.

"I'm a...consultant," he drawled.

Lindsay's nose crinkled as she eyed him, taking in his attire. He'd switched out his leather vest for his leather jacket. He wore black biker boots, black jeans, and a black T-shirt. The patches might as well have been neon signs. "You must not be a very good one."

Smoke squeezed my hand again and tugged, causing me to look at him. He was smiling at Lindsay. I recognized that smile—a cat playing with a bird before it pounced. I settled back into my chair.

"I'm very good at what I do, Lindsay. And it pays very well. I also believe in that old saying—what you see is what you get." His gaze flicked to Justin. "Unlike some people."

Lindsay being Lindsay couldn't let it go. I finally diverted her attention by pumping for her information about the wedding—ostensibly the reason for this dinner meet-up. And, Lindsay being Lindsay, she took that conversational bull by the horns and ran with it.

The waiter returned and asked about dessert. Smoke ordered Boston Creme Pie without asking but he flashed me one of those "trust-me" looks he was becoming famous for. I'd never had it but from the description in the dessert menu—white cake, vanilla creme filling, chocolate icing? Oh, yeah. I was all over that. I still wanted to know why it was called pie, though. While we waited for dessert to be served, Lindsay demanded I go to the bathroom with her.

Smoke stood, held my chair. Justin sprawled in his chair pretty much ignoring my sister. She huffed at him and pushed against his chair to squeeze past. Smoke dropped a kiss on the back of my neck as I edged past him and I had the sudden urge to forget dessert and just go home.

"More fun with Dick and Jane," he murmured just loud enough for me to hear.

I choked, barely managing to cover my laugh. Lindsay leveled a scorching glare on me so I meekly followed her to the ladies room.

The door hadn't shut all the way before she whirled to face me. Her stormy expression was just the precursor.

"How could you!" she demanded.

I dropped onto the cushy couch, leaned back, and crossed my legs and arms.

Lindsay scowled, her rant disrupted by my actions. "What are you doing?"

"I'm settling in for the tantrum."

If she'd been a cartoon character, steam would be coming from her ears.

"You are not funny, Leigh. How could

you embarrass me in front of Justin like this?"

"How did I embarrass you, Lindsay? Oh...you mean because my boyfriend knows more about wine than yours?"

"No! Wait. Boyfriend? Since when do you have a boyfriend?"

Her tone insinuated that I was somehow incapable of getting and/or keeping one. "Since I met Smoke."

"Smoke?" She sneered. "What kind of name is that? And what does he really do for a living?"

Sadly, I didn't have real answers to those questions, but I could ad lib with the best. "Smoke is his kind of name and just what he said. He's a consultant. Like a troubleshooter." Yeah. He'd told me he worked for the Nightrider's national president as a troubleshooter. At the time, I'd quipped something stupid like, "Yeah? So when there's trouble, he sends you in to shoot it?" I'd laughed but he'd turned serious, shaking his head. "No. That's why he has Gravedigger." I'd shut up after that and never asked again. Now I was having to defend him against my sister.

"He's probably one of your criminals and you just made him come so you could embarrass Justin! And me!" That last word turned into a wail and crocodile tears welled in her eyes.

"Jeez, Lindsay. Stop being such a drama queen." I pushed off the couch and strode to the door. The shocked look on her face was sadly satisfying. What did that say about me as a sister?

I wolfed down my dessert, ignored the coffee and was all but bouncing in my chair from the urge to leave. When the bills finally arrived, Smoke snatched both from under Justin's hand. Man, he had some quick reflexes. He took a cursory look at the total, reached into his pocket and pulled out several hundred-dollar bills. When the waiter returned, Smoke placed a single hundred on the tray with the bill for the wine he'd ordered. "For the sommelier," Smoke told him.

The waiter had already tallied up the tip on his tray and he smiled at Smoke. "Of course, sir. Thank you for your patronage."

I could not get out of that place fast enough. While we waited for my Highlander to be brought up by the valet, Smoke pulled me into his arms and kissed me. Hard. Leaving me breathless. And really sorry we'd had dessert instead of going home.

Bang. Bang-bang-bang! BANG!

EIGHT

Smoke

I HEARD THE HARLEY gunning down the street and took Leigh to the ground as five shots rang out. I kicked the feet out from under the valet standing there with his mouth hanging open. Fortunately, the doorman was quick on the uptake and had the people in line behind us safely back inside the building.

To say I was pissed was an understatement. I wanted to shift to track the fucker, but my wolf was dead set on staying with Leigh. He reminded me that we had an audience and shifting into wolf form would not be a smart idea. I didn't let her up until I was sure a second attack wasn't coming. By then, sirens were echoing off the buildings as flashing lights painted their facades. Three cop cars skidded to a stop in front of the restaurant.

My first instinct was to dismiss the shooting as kids and firecrackers when the cops asked. Too bad the gunman had hit the building. Evidence like that couldn't be ignored. As I figured they would, the cops separated me from Leigh. I leaned up against one of the squad cars, ankles crossed, thumbs hooked in my front pockets, and watched her. When she got wound up, she got animated. Her hands flicked and flailed. I didn't need to hear her—I could of course, but her expression said everything I needed to know. The fact she was "on the job" helped slightly but the cops sure didn't like the idea of her being with me. Tough shit. She was mine.

I answered questions—barely. Most of my attention was focused on the shooter and the biker. There'd been two—one driving, one on the back firing. Neither had been wearing colors. If they'd been Hell Dogs, they would have circled around to make sure of the kill. I didn't want to think about the alternative. A real Nightrider wouldn't go after a brother this way, would never disgrace his cut like this. But there were all those hang-arounds congregating with Boner. I needed to find out a hellava lot more about the president of the Dallas chapter.

It was midnight before the cops turned us loose. I put Leigh to bed, planning to wait until she was asleep before heading to the Dallas clubhouse. We'd just settled in when her cell phone rang. She popped up like she was on a spring.

"Daniels."

I listened to both sides of the conversation. Ah, the perks of being a Wolf. There was another fire. She ordered me to stay put as she jerked on coveralls and shoved her feet into boots. Her kit was already stashed in the FD sedan parked out front.

She stuffed her phone in a chest pocket and turned to me. "Not sure when I'll get back. I'll probably go straight to the arson office once I'm clear of the scene. I'll see you back here for dinner tonight?"

I grabbed the coveralls by the unzipped plackets and hauled her to me. Kissing her hard, she was breathless when I let her go. "Take care of you."

Spinning her around, I sent her toward the bedroom door with a pat on her ass. She glanced back, laughing and rolling her eyes. "You know, there's just something surreal about going off to a fire scene after getting kissed by a naked man."

She was still laughing when she closed and locked the front door. I was two minutes behind her but being on a bike meant I'd beat her there. I needed to check it out before too many other scents fucked things up.

I shifted near the scene and it didn't take me long to locate the arsonist's trail coming and going from the building. He'd used a vacant lot and some trees for cover. I tracked him going toward the building but one of the firefighters saw me and yelled. I ducked away, trying to act like a dog.

Cutting through the empty lot, I discovered the Nightrider cut—with my name sewn on it—hidden in the weeds where it would be found come daylight. I also located where the asshole had parked. From the tire treads, probably a pickup. I had his personal scent now. He smelled of stale beer, marijuana, and gasoline, with an underlying layer of stagnant water. I'd be able to pick him out of a crowd and that's what I aimed to do.

It was way past time to pay the Dallas clubhouse another visit.

🐾 🐾 🐾 🐾

Leigh

THIS WAS THE FOURTH warehouse fire in this area in the past month. I leaned against the district chief's car and watched the guys put up a defensive fight. There was no reason for them to make an interior push and chance getting hurt if the roof or a wall collapsed. They already had a good knockdown on it, and I was pretty sure I'd find some evidence once I got access.

I yawned just as the chief's driver walked up. He had a Styrofoam cup in each hand and offered me one. I sniffed. Coffee. Great. I needed the caffeine.

"I have creamer and sugar in my pocket," he offered.

Taking a sip, I nodded. "This is fresh. but I like a little sweet. One packet will do me." He passed it over, I dumped it in and used the folded-up paper to stir. I took another sip. Good enough.

One of the guys yelled, and I looked up just in time to see a large dog run into the weeds of the lot next door. The thing looked familiar, but I couldn't figure out why. I didn't make it a habit of hanging out in this part of Dallas. An industrial area on the decline, I made a note to check on owners, mortgage holders, lessees—anyone who could profit by having the place burned out. I added real estate developers to my list. I didn't think this area was a candidate for redevelopment, but what did I know?

About two hours after I hit the scene, the chief cleared me to enter the warehouse and came with me. As I'd anticipated, the damage wasn't too bad. I swept the beam of my flashlight across the space, highlighting a stack of stuff. I exchanged a look with him. "Better notify the cops. They'll want to see this."

I stared at bundles that stank like marijuana and other brick-sized lumps wrapped in plastic and duct tape. There was paraphernalia that had to be drug related. "Do you think they were cooking meth?" That meant we'd have to call the HazMat team and go through decontamination.

"Naw. No glass jars or tubing. I think this was a distribution center, that's all."

Poking through the debris, I glimpsed some melted plastic with wires. A trigger? I traded Latex gloves for my work gloves and poked at the device. A twinge of recognition niggled the back of my memory. I opened my evidence kit and using large tweezers, dug the thing out and placed it in an evidence bag. I'd have to do some research. For the first time, I thought I might have a handle on the arsonist. Drugs. Did the guy have a vendetta against drugs? Or was this something a bit more incendiary, like war between dealers and their gangs? I for sure needed to hook up with my cop buddies.

🐾 🐾 🐾 🐾

Smoke

I RODE UP to the clubhouse and got a sneer from the provisional—a human—guarding the gate. Yeah, the Russian and Gravedigger needed to pay these assholes and their president a visit. Soon.

Parking my bike, I strolled inside like I owned the place. My wolf was bigger and badder than Boner's so I could challenge but who wanted the hassle? Not me. That's why my cut said NOMAD. Boner sat in a chair that looked a lot like a throne. A topless woman occupied one arm of the chair while a second woman's head bobbed up and down in the bastard's lap.

Sex in the clubhouse was a given and I could mostly ignore it. I preferred my fucking private but far be it for me to harass a brother for getting his rocks off. The problem as I saw it was that these were the only two females present and everyone else was standing there watching—like they'd been ordered to. Sick bastard.

I headed to the bar and grabbed a beer from the cooler, twisted off the cap then headed back outside. Bikes weren't the only vehicles in the lot, and I wanted to check out a pickup I'd seen tucked back in the shadows.

Sure enough, the treads matched but the only scent I could pick up was gasoline and ammonia. Even as good as my nose was, I couldn't penetrate the overwhelming stench. That was fine. I had other ways to track—like the small GPS device in my pocket. I slapped it under the back bumper and wandered back into the clubhouse. The show was over, and the brothers had bellied up to the bar. The two sweet butts were serving drinks.

Boner caught my eye and waved me toward the backroom he used as an office. This would be fun. As I stepped through the door, a shape rushed me from the left. I ducked, twisted, and put my shoulder into the guy's solar plexus with enough force to empty his lungs. I dumped him on the floor and stamped my boot on his throat.

I growled, "Move and I'll break your neck." I didn't look at him. I was too busy staring down Boner. Shit. I needed backup. Like yesterday. I slammed the door and locked it. That would keep any but the most determined of his people out. The guy under my boot was not a Wolf. Had he been, we'd still be fighting.

"What the fuck, Boner."

"If you think you can walk in here and take over, asshole, you're wrong."

Laughing, I shook my head at his idiocy. "You see the back of my cut? I'm a lone Wolf, you asshole. I don't want your fucking chapter." I wanted to throw the Russian in his face, but I couldn't tip my hand—not this early in the game. Not until I knew what was happening and had something solid to report. But I was starting to wonder. Were the Nightriders getting set up by Hell Dogs or by men who were supposed to be brothers? And where were the drugs getting roasted in the arson fires coming from?

"I know who you are, fucker. The gawddamned Russian holds your leash. You tell 'im that if he wants me, he can come challenge me his own damn self."

Yeah, I wouldn't have to worry about Boner too much longer. He'd just signed his own death warrant. I held my hands out, splayed at waist level in a conciliatory gesture. "Ease down, dude. Since when was a brother on the road not welcome in a chapter clubhouse?"

"My clubhouse, my rules."

"Whatever, Boner. I'm outta here." I glanced down at the hanger-on under my boot. "Don't move." His eyes were wide as he blinked in acknowledgment. Boner growled something about him being a pussy. Better a live pussy than a dead idiot.

I put my boot on the floor, pivoted and opened the door. A couple more humans stood there, trying to look mean. I let my wolf out to play—just enough for them to see the predator in my expression. They all but pissed themselves getting out of my way. A couple of the brothers offered quick nods as I passed. Good to know at least some had my back.

Six blocks away, I pulled into a convenience store. Five minutes later, two brothers rode up. We nodded a greeting and waited in silence. Another five passed then a solitary rider arrived—Rook, Boner's VP.

"We need to talk."

Yeah, no shit.

NINE

Smoke

I HEADED to Leigh's house about noon. I figured she'd still be at work and I wanted some down time to do some planning. No fuckin' way I'd go back to sleeping at the Dallas clubhouse—not after my little run-in with Boner. He'd probably try to slit my throat while I slept. Not that he was capable enough to sneak up on me.

The POS red sedan was absent when I pulled up at the condo. I'd have a couple of hours to touch base with The Russian and see about getting some back-up in place, in case I needed it. My cell buzzed as I walked through the front door. Leigh.

"Hey, babe."

"Where are you?"

"You're place. You comin' home?"

I could almost feel her deep sigh through the cell. "I wish. I have to go see some cops about the drug warehouse that burned last night."

"Fun times." Not. And I had to admit I wasn't thrilled with the idea of Leigh dragging the cops into this situation.

"Um…Smoke?"

Something in her tone was off. "What?"

"Can I ask you a question?"

Shit. "Yeah." Just because she asked didn't mean I'd answer.

Another sigh, and this one went straight to my dick. "Do you...I mean..."

"Spit it out, babe." I had an idea where she was headed.

"You don't...*use*, do you?" She sounded small and uncertain and like she hated to ask. Thank fuck.

"No." I answered swift and sure. I didn't use that crap. Some of the brothers did, not that there was any lasting effect. Wolf physiology and metabolism burned that shit up. We didn't get high. Same with alcohol and cigarettes. We did those because we liked the taste.

She let out a relieved breath. "Okay. Good. But...um...do you, by chance, maybe know..."

"I don't know the players in Dallas, babe. I could ask around if that's what you want." Not that I would. I knew exactly who the players were. Hell Dogs, a couple of gangs—black and Hispanic, and the local Nightriders. Boner had never been one to expand. The Dallas club had two sources of income—running drug shipments and the chop shop that operated under the guise of the salvage yard. Bloody short-sighted if you asked me.

"Would you?"

"For you, babe? Sure."

I wondered again where those stashes of

drugs had come from. That was a big hit to the cash flow for someone. And if this whole thing was some stupid Boner plan? Who was he stealing the drugs from? If he stole from the wrong people, it would come back to bite us all in the ass eventually.

I dialed the Russian. We had a lot to discuss.

🐾 🐾 🐾 🐾

Leigh

"WE GOT A TIP on the hotline." My boss, Captain Fielder, stuck his head around the wall of my cubicle. He was no relation to the baseball player but the two could pass for brothers. Like Prince, the captain was large and affable with a complexion the color of acorns.

"Yeah?"

He handed me a sheet of paper. "Yeah. Someone saw two people at the scene. A guy in a red pickup truck and a guy on a Harley." I didn't breathe for a minute, then remembered Smoke had been with me.

"Descriptions?" We couldn't get that lucky, but I crossed mental fingers, just in case.

"Older pickup, probably a Dodge. Red. Parked about a block away in a mostly dirt and gravel parking lot. He sat there in the truck until the Harley arrived."

"The witness is sure it was a Harley?"

The captain lowered his chin and stared at her. "As the witness said, nothing sounds like a Harley."

I thought about Smoke's Harley. Yeah, even when tuned correctly, there was just something that set a Harley engine apart.

"Pickup guy was early twenties, with a beard. He wore a black jacket and jeans. Harley guy was older, maybe mid-thirties or forties. He wore a black vest."

My chest constricted. "Anything on the jacket or vest?"

Fielder gave me a sharp look. "No. Plain. Where are you going with that thought?"

"Evidently nowhere. Anything else?"

"They talked, a box exchanged hands, the motorcycle left, and pickup guy headed in the direction of the warehouse on foot."

"Please tell me the witness got a tag number?"

"Nope."

Dammit. No way we could get that lucky. Still, we had some descriptions. I yawned, not quite hiding it fast enough.

"Go home, Daniels. Get some sleep."

He didn't have to tell me twice.

Smoke wasn't around so I kicked off my boots and flopped face down in bed, my need for sleep overriding my need for food. He'd wake me when he got home, we'd eat, and maybe I'd get lucky. I laughed. There was no *maybe* about it. With Smoke, I *always* got lucky. I yawned and snuggled into the pillow that carried the scent of leather and cherry pipe tobacco.

A muffled voice coaxed me awake. I started to smile because it was dark, and Smoke was home. Then I caught what he was saying.

"Sooner or later, boss. Boner is a problem that needs to be fixed." Smoke didn't say anything for a minute or so. "Yeah. I have a lead I plan to check out. Someone is fuckin' with us with these fires and it needs to stop." More silence as he listened, and then, "I told you I'd checked all the scenes. I'm the best arsonist you have, Russki. That's why you sent me down here."

Listening, I caught a rustling sound, like denim brushing on denim, but I kept my eyes closed and feigned sleep, despite my heart wanting to explode from my chest. I had to keep it together, to stay calm even as my brain whirled. I sensed that Smoke was looming over the bed, staring at me. Then his fingertips brushed through my hair and I had to concentrate to keep from reacting.

What was going on? Who was this *boss* Smoke was talking to? Then his words sank in. He'd just admitted he was an arsonist and it hit me. Smoke. His road name. Was he *my* arsonist? I focused on keeping my heart rate and breathing normal. He was too close. *Breathe*, I reminded my lungs as he moved away.

"I said I'd take care of it." He was growling at the caller. "I have Leigh under control. She won't be a problem."

I held my breath, waiting, but he was gone. I was cold inside. Smoke was involved with my cases. Somehow. I was sick to my stomach. What would he do if he discovered I'd overheard him? Because Smoke Jenner was a very, very bad man.

Straining to hear, I caught the soft snick of the front door. I sprang out of bed and grabbed my boots. Not feeling a bit guilty, I shoved the hurt welling up in my chest away and focused. If Smoke was involved, if he was using me and only pretending to care about me, the sooner I knew about it, the better. I'd deal with the pain and fallout later.

I took my Highlander. There were thousands of the same model in the metroplex. Smoke would be far less likely to notice my tail than he would if I drove my FD sedan. Besides, my Highlander was in perfect mechanical shape. The last thing I needed was to get stranded on the side of the road. That's what got me into this mess in the first place.

Smoke was in a hurry, but he obeyed traffic laws and speed limits. He switched from city streets to I-35E and headed north. Was he leaving town? My heart stuttered and I chastised my idiocy. Smoke was…smoke. Here today, gone tomorrow. I'd known better than to get seriously involved with him. His last words played on a loop in my head. Under control? I'd show him who was under control.

He exited the interstate and I realized we were headed toward Lewisville Lake. Why would he be coming out here? I had to drop back because traffic turned sporadic. It took me awhile, but I finally found his Harley— parked behind an old red pickup. Son of a bitch. I caught movement on a private dock, a faintly Smoke-shaped shadow headed toward a large wooden boathouse.

I hid my Highlander where it couldn't be seen from the boathouse and got out. Using the shadows just like Smoke had, I stalked to the structure. I tried to peek in through a dirty window but could see nothing. When I got to the door, it was open. I crouched down and slipped through so I wouldn't be silhouetted. With my back to the wall, I straightened slowly, my fingers searching for the light switch. When I found it, I flipped it on. A single 40-watt bulb in the center of the place struggled to illuminate the corners. Smoke stood on the other side of the boat slip, a body at his feet.

🐾

Smoke

"GET OUT." Fuck. I did not need this. Bad enough my suspect was dead. Other than his truck being at the Dallas clubhouse, I had no way to tie him to Boner. And now Leigh was here. And pissed. How the hell had she found me? I'd left her sleeping, except my wolf had been trying to get my attention. Shit. She hadn't been asleep at all. And I'd been so focused on finding my prey that I hadn't considered a tail.

She stared, horrified even as an argument formed on the lips I wanted to kiss. Fisted hands planted on her hips and her chin jutted, she furrowed her brows until a tight vee formed. "No way I'm leaving. What have you done?"

When I didn't answer, she marched around the dock and stopped in front of me. I wanted to kiss the crinkled skin just above the bridge of her nose despite the situation. I gestured at what was stacked along the walls. "It's not safe, babe."

She glanced around then, eyes widening as they adjusted to the gloom in the boat house and she recognized the markings on the crates and boxes. "What the hell?"

"Yeah. Exactly." The place was stacked to the rafters with explosive material, all rigged to blow. My nose had already cataloged the various types.

"Oh, crap."

"You can say that again."

"Oh, crap."

"Funny."

"Wasn't meant to be. What do we do now?"

"*We* don't do anything. *You're* leaving." I put command in my voice, like she'd pay any attention. Still, worth a shot. She needed to get the hell away from here.

"Seriously? You really think I'm under your control?"

Well shit. She definitely hadn't been sleeping.

"You think you can scare me away so can get rid of the evidence? Not happening. You're under arrest for murder."

"Don't fucking argue, babe. You need to get out of here."

"No. We'll both get out after I handcuff you, then I'll call the bomb squad, and they will come do their job by dealing with the explosives."

I pointed to a digital timer happily counting down. "Too late."

Her eyes widened as she studied the device. "You started it. You can just stop it."

"Except I didn't."

Something in my expression made her backpedal. She gulped, cleared her throat before asking, "Did I set it off? But how? I didn't touch anything."

"Probably happened when I walked in. Vibrations on the floor started the countdown, or there's a pressure plate." I hunkered down next to the device. "If the room starts shaking, you need to run like hell."

"If the room shakes, we're toast."

She was right but I wasn't about to admit defeat. I pulled a multi-tool from my back pocket and set to work.

"What are you doing?" Leigh didn't quite screech but the timbre of her voice hurt my ears.

"My job."

"Your job? You're an arsonist. You burn

stuff down." Was she scoffing? Little did she know. I'd just have to prove it to her.

"Sometimes. Wasn't always. I was Marine Force Recon, EOD tech." As an Explosive Ordinance Disposal tech, I'd disabled or blown up a shit-ton of IEDs in the sandbox. I never figured I'd be sitting in a fancy boathouse on Lake Lewisville sweating bullets as I worked to save my ass. And Leigh's. Especially hers. I had plans for that sweet ass that didn't include it getting blown to hell and back.

"Wait. You were a marine?"

I cut my eyes her direction. She looked stunned. "Yeah. Proud member of Uncle Sam's Misguided Children."

"But..." She waved her hands like she couldn't figure out the next word. One waved at my head, the other at the rest of me. Shrugging, I turned back to the bomb.

"Walk soft, babe, but go stand by the door." She hovered for a few moments, peering over my shoulder. I grunted and shifted back on my heels. "Now, Leigh. If we have to evacuate, I want you where I can grab you on the way out. Yeah?"

"Yeah, no." She placed a hand on my shoulder and leaned to get a better look.

"If you're the Ghost, that's not your trigger. Can you disarm it? I mean...no pressure or anything."

I turned my head and stole a kiss. "Yeah, no pressure."

She breathed heavily, air brushing

across the side of my neck, then straightened. Finally. She did as I asked, pussyfooting to the door leading to the dock. I studied a tangle of wires and the trigger device. Leigh was right. This wasn't my design. Dammit. Nothing could be easy, and Luck was being a bitch tonight.

I studied the wiring. "Just want you to know, babe, I didn't do this. Any of it."

"Then tell me what's going on."

"Yeah...no. Can't do that."

"Then you *are* guilty." At least she sounded sort of disappointed.

"Nope. I'm not. Someone is trying to set up my club." I could give her that much. She'd have to take the rest on faith. My wolf waited for her to decide.

"Why should I believe you?"

I paused again but didn't look at her. "Either you do, or you don't, babe."

"Are we going to die?"

"Not if I can help it."

I concentrated on the timer and Leigh stayed silent. For about sixty seconds.

"You're hot, you know. Like setting me on fire hot."

I froze then glanced over my shoulder. I arched my right brow and she waggled hers at me in some sort of flirty semaphore I had no clue how to read. "Not the time, babe."

"It is. Just in case. I...wanted you to know. I'll be your match and you can light my fire."

"Uh huh." I bent back to the job at hand,

but she kept talking.

"I'll light up your life."

I clipped a wire. "That's a bad love song, ba—"

The timer went dark as sparks shot out. "Fuck!" I was up and running, barreling into Leigh, through her and the door, turning at the last minute so my back hit the dock railing. I curled around her as the explosives erupted, raining fire and fury on us. We hit the surface of the lake. Went under. Deep.

When we came up for air, Leigh pushed sopping hair out of her eyes, grinning like some evil jack-o-lantern. "Smoke on the water. Speaking of bad love songs."

TEN

Leigh

SMOKE SWAM like a stinking fish. I floundered along, wishing I wasn't wearing my duty boots. After circling me like a shark focused on dinner, he moved in.

"Lay back and relax, babe."

The next thing I knew, he had an arm over my shoulder and across my chest in a classic lifeguard hold and was swimming away from the shattered boathouse. I did as he suggested—relaxed.

After a minute or so, I jumped right into the conversation I didn't want to have. "So...who was the dead guy?"

"No clue."

"Was he dead when you found him?"

"D'uh."

"Don't get snippy."

"Don't interrogate me. You've already accused me of murder and arson." He continued to stroke steadily, and I realized we were getting further and further away from the scene—and my car!

"Wait! You're going the wrong way. We have to go back. I need to report in. I—"

"No, babe." His words were quiet but

forceful.

"What do you mean no?"

"I mean you need to stay out of this. These guys are playing for keeps, babe, and they won't hesitate to take out a civilian."

"I'm not a *civilian,* Smoke." I put as much emphasis and derision as I could into that word. "I'm an arson investigator. In case you haven't noticed."

That hot fudge laugh of his rolled over me. "Trust me, I've noticed."

"This is my job. I need to get back there, talk to the cops and FD so they call the bomb squad. Or the ATF."

"You don't want the feds involved." His voice was still quiet but that almost sounded like a threat.

"I want whoever is behind these fires. They have to be stopped before some other innocent person gets hurt."

"Trust me, babe. He wasn't innocent."

"I thought you didn't know who he is."

"I don't know his name. I do know what he is. Or was."

"Same thing." I huffed it out, grouchy at his semantics.

"Nope. Not even close."

After that, no matter what I tried, he ignored me. I knew one surefire way to get his attention, but he wisely kept that part of his anatomy out of reach. After what seemed like an hour, but was probably only fifteen minutes, he stopped swimming. Moments later, my feet could reach the lake bottom and then I was glad I was wearing my boots, despite them being full of water.

We lurched up on the narrow beach and I looked around for human habitation. There was none. To the north—or what I presumed was north, I could still see flames dancing, along with flashing emergency lights, at the marina.

Smoke found a concrete bench and nudged me down on it. He stripped my Ropers, poured water out then peeled off my socks and twisted them between his hands to wring out more water. He left them to me to pull back on while he dealt with his own boots.

Ugh. There is nothing slimier—or harder—than pulling on wet socks. I pushed my feet into my boots and stood. At least I didn't squish when I walked. If we had to hoof it all the way back to the marina, I'd have a bumper crop of blisters.

I watched him and wondered. Did I believe him? Some instinct I couldn't name insisted he was telling the truth—that he *was* innocent. Too bad I had no evidence. I wanted to think the worst of him. He was a freaking outlaw biker. If my suspicions were correct, he was a major arsonist dozens of agencies were still looking for. But he was Smoke. *My* Smoke. The man who made me omelets—after breaking into my house. The man who covered me with his body when someone shot at us. He was right. The bad guys were playing for keeps. But what color hat did he wear?

"This way." Smoke's quiet command cut into the circular argument clogging up my mind.

"Where are we going?"

And...he didn't say a word—just started walking. We were back to the silent treatment again. I followed him, leaving a trail of water dripping from my coveralls. We walked up on his Harley, parked in the shadows of a nearby building.

"Get on."

"I want my car."

"I'll arrange for it."

He pulled a phone out of a compartment on his motorcycle and walked away. I reached into my chest pocket to grab my own phone. Two people could play this game...except my phone was in no condition to make a call. I tried to remember what the Internet said to do with a wet phone. Rice. Yeah, I didn't think there was enough rice in the world to dry my phone. Still...I'd make Smoke stop on the way home so I could get some.

🐾 🐾 🐾 🐾

Smoke

I PARKED behind a convenience store and waited. About ten minutes later, two brothers rode up on one bike. They were Wolves and I trusted them, where I didn't trust many of the others in the local chapter. I handed over a copy of the keyless start fob for Leigh's SUV.

She watched the hand-off but had no clue that I'd cloned her fob. No reason to break into the Toyota and hot wire it when I could take care of it the easy—if slightly illegal way. When she got up in the morning, her Highlander would be parked in its normal spot.

"I need rice," she said as I walked back.

"For?"

She held up her cell phone. I managed to keep a straight face when I said, "Not enough rice in China, babe. I'll buy you a new one."

"I don't want a new one," she gritted out. "This one has all my info."

"You have it backed up on your laptop. I'll buy you a new one, you can download it. Done deal."

She snarled at me, but her argument was invalid and she knew it.

"Who were those guys and what did you give them?"

"Brothers and directions to find your vehicle." She gave me a squinty-eyed look and I laughed. "Just trust me, babe."

And speaking of trust, I backed away and gave her a squinty-eyed look of my own. She knew I was an arsonist. Said as much back there in the boathouse. That wasn't common knowledge. I'd never been arrested—too good a covering my tracks. She had to be guessing that I was the Ghost, but I needed to find out.

"Why do you think I'm the Ghost?"

Her mouth opened and closed a few times and I got distracted thinking about how good her lips would feel wrapped around my dick.

"Ummm." She was stalling. I crossed my arms over my chest. "Lucky guess?"

"Babe." Lucky guess my ass.

She leaned in and looked up at me, batting her eyelashes and puckering her lips.

"Are you trying to distract me, Leigh?"

Her hand cupped me as she flashed me a sultry smile. "No."

I pulled away from her. "Answer my question."

"What's the point?"

I glanced down, stared. Seconds later, she slugged me.

"Eyes up, dude."

I swear I wasn't looking there. I tend to stare at my boots when I'm thinking, and I was thinking pretty damn hard at the moment. She thought I was all about her tits. Well, I was, but I'm a guy. We're always all about tits. At the moment, though, hers weren't the top thing on my mind. Still, two could play sex games.

"When I drive *that* point home, babe, you'll be all over me like—"

"Shut up, Smoke."

I didn't reply. She lasted about 45 seconds. "So, what *is* the point, if not..." She waved a hand in the area of my belt buckle.

"The question is exactly the point. I want to know where you got your info." Her lips thinned as she turned stubborn. Then something else occurred. I studied her, curious now. "Why you?"

"Why me what?"

"Back at the boathouse, you said that wasn't my trigger, wasn't the Ghost's. Why would you recognize the Ghost's trigger? And why would you automatically link me to him?" I was pretty damn sure *I* wasn't on anyone's radar. The Ghost? That was an altogether different situation.

She dug her boot toe in the dirt and wouldn't meet my eyes. "Cold case I was researching. The arsonist used a trigger like the one I found at the warehouse fire." She pursed her lips, glanced up and looked me right in the eye. "The one where you showed up after I almost hit that dog..." Her voice trailed off and she looked speculative.

"I didn't set that fire, Leigh." Her scowl deepened. "I was there, yeah, but after it started." I studied her and her gaze skittered away. "So you put two and two together about the triggers." I sighed inwardly. She was not going to let this go. "I'm not the Ghost, babe. And I don't have a signature MO." I did—from my days in the sandbox but that was then. "I also don't do arson for hire." Or for fun. I wasn't a firebug—not in the psychological sense. Arson was club business.

"You have a fan club."

I stared at her. Talk about a *non-sequitur* shift of topic.

"Seriously. On the 'net. There are fan sites and your name kept coming up. Well, not *your* name but The Ghost's." She made air quote marks with her fingers and emphasized the name like both words were capitalized. "They say no one ever died at your hands. That you were an avenger for justice."

I sobered. "I've killed, babe. Plenty of times."

"But that was war, right? When you were a marine?"

"This is war too."

"Swear to me, Smoke. Swear you aren't part of this case."

"I didn't start the fires, but I'm involved. Those assholes dragged me in."

She rubbed her hands down the wet material hugging her thighs. Then her chin came up as if she'd made a decision. "Okay then. Let's go catch the bad guys."

Yeah, they were dead men walking.

ELEVEN

Leigh

I FELT LIKE a total sleaze as I handed over the fingerprint I'd lifted from a glass Smoke drank from at my house. I'd just spent two hours getting the down and dirty on the local biker gangs. The Nightriders weren't a huge presence. They had about twenty members and were small-time drug runners for some of the cartels and were on Auto Theft's radar because of a salvage yard they owned. Another motorcycle gang, the Hell Dogs, seemed to be testing the waters. They had a major impact in south Texas. They ran a major prostitution ring, drugs, guns, and if rumor was correct, murder for hire. Awesome.

Smoke made no bones about being an outlaw biker. I knew I was walking a very thin line by getting involved with him, but I just couldn't stay away. The man was far too sexy, and I sensed something honorable about him. Totally weird, but still. Given all the evidence to the contrary, my heart trusted him on an instinctual level. That scared me.

Then to discover that my suspicions about his arson expertise were correct? When I'd tossed out that I knew he was an arsonist,

I'd expected his patented "Babe." I didn't get that. I got that he'd been an EOD tech in the Marines and following the logic, I'd come to the conclusion that he was more than likely the serial arsonist the Internet called "The Ghost."

All I knew was that he called himself Smoke, his last name was Jenner and he'd once been a marine. I wanted to know everything. Every wart. So I sneaked the fingerprint and took it to the lab after I canvassed my buddies in the DPD gang unit with some general questions about the culture and criminal footprint of all the motorcycle gangs in the area.

"Got a hit," the fingerprint tech announced.

"That was quick."

"The guy's in the military database."

The printer started up so I moved over the check the pages it was spitting out. I gathered the stack of paper and thanked everyone. I needed some quiet time to digest the information I'd just received on Mastery Gunnery Sergeant Brian Jenner, former Marine hero, current outlaw biker aka Smoke. He hadn't lied about his identity.

I walked into my cubby and dropped the fat file on my desk. My phone was lit up like a Las Vegas casino. I punched in and started listening to voice mail. What had Smoke told me? Oh, yeah. He wasn't on anyone's radar. Wrong. The ATF wanted immediate access to me, my investigation, and Smoke.

Before I could get up and disappear, Fielder arrived with three guys in tow. I recognized one of them. He and I had worked a case two years ago. The ATF had arrived. Yippee.

🐾 🐾 🐾 🐾

Smoke

I STOOD in the back of the smoke-filled club. The manager obviously didn't give a damn about clean air laws. The cell phone in my hip pocket buzzed. I jerked it out and put it to my ear.

"Damn, Smoke. What's up with all that racket?" Hardy—short for Hardass—Tyree, the Nightriders national vice president, yelled in my ear.

"Had a tip. Hang on."

I pushed through the crowd toward the exit. The place was way over the fire marshal's limit too. Outside in the humid night air, the bass from the band was a throbbing reminder of the party going on inside.

"What's up, Hardy?"

"You said you had a tip?"

I knuckled my temple, hoping the raging headache would disappear now that I was removed from the noise. "Yeah. There's a rumor that this place is next on the list. I wanted to check it out."

"And?"

"Nothin'."

"The Dallas chapter have anything to say?"

"Not a fuckin' word. Boner is keeping a tight leash, especially on the brothers I trust. The new guys? The humans? They're as clueless as the rest of us. That's not good. This is their territory." My eyes roamed the parking lot, catching each movement and shadow. I was a predator, pure and simple. "I don't get it. The Nightriders don't own any of the properties that have been torched. There's barely a whiff of Hell Dogs anywhere. When I first came down, I couldn't figure out why I was here."

"And now?"

"Someone knows I'm around. They're using my former MO to set the fires. There aren't many around who know, Hardy."

"You need backup? We don't like the direction Boner is headed."

"Neither do I. He's involved, somehow. Could he have sold us out to the Hell Dogs?"

"The Russian will roast his balls and feed them to the crows if he has."

I figured as much. "I'm good for now. If I need cover, I'll call in."

"What about the girl?"

Shit. He was talking about Leigh. I didn't know how to answer. As I was working up a reply, a muffled boom which was immediately followed by screams scrambled my thoughts. "Oh, fuck no." I was running toward the door before my brain caught up to my feet. "Gotta go."

I shoved the phone back into my pocket. The exit door—the one I'd left *unlocked* when I walked out—was jammed shut. "Fuck!"

I grabbed the handle and jerked. Metal groaned. My shoulders bunched as I used my foot to brace while I yanked again. The door gave and I almost ended up on my butt. Regaining my balance, I reached in and started pulling people out.

Wolf hearing is sensitive, and I picked up electrical pops and whooshing flames beneath the cacophony of screams. Clearing the bottleneck at the door, I forced my way inside. I needed to get people out. Fast. The old building was a tinderbox.

I made the rounds. All the fucking doors were locked. People had piled up at the blocked fire doors. More code violations. I kicked exits open and terrified clubbers spilled out into the night, walls of flame chasing them. Black spots swam in front of my eyes and my lungs burned like a sonavabitch. I tripped over one last victim on my way out—one of the waitresses. Tossing her over my shoulder, I bulled my way to the back door, passing firefighters on the way in. One took the unconscious girl from me.

I needed to get the hell away from there. I was already a suspect in the other fires, despite Leigh saying she thought I was innocent. From the number of fire apparatus in the parking lot, I figured the fire had gone 3-alarm at least. I made it about ten feet away from my bike when a conversation caught my attention.

Two men, crouched down behind a pickup truck. They stank of booze, drugs, and black powder. They were human.

"What happened?"

"Somebody unlocked the doors."

"We need to..." Sirens obscured the conversation—even from my enhanced hearing. "...we have the remedy. I'll take..."

I didn't hear the rest. Someone took me face-first to the ground, handcuffing my hands behind my back. I cranked my head around to look up. Leigh stood in front of me.

"Brian Jenner, you're under arrest."

Well, fuck.

TWELVE

Smoke

I WAS IN a hellava bind but some perverse streak made me rock up to my knees. The cops surrounding me tensed, and one kept a hand hovering over the butt of his gun. Not that it mattered much. Even with my hands cuffed behind my back, I could take them down. Hell, I could even if I wasn't a Wolf. All that training forced on Uncle Sam's Misguided Children didn't evaporate once the uniforms were packed away.

"This what you been dreamin' about, babe?" I dropped my voice to a low purr. "Me on my knees, waiting for your orders?" I was no fucking submissive but from the fiery color flooding her cheeks and the splash of her geranium and clove scent drenched in damp heat? Yeah, I wondered if maybe Leigh didn't have at least some curiosity. I'd be happy to explore those things with her—once I got out of this mess.

"Shut up, Smo—" She choked off my name and cleared her throat. "*Err*, Mr. Jenner."

"Babe."

Her hands fisted and she looked ready to

slug me. "What were you doing here tonight?"

"You gonna do this right here?"

"Yes."

"Can I get off the fucking pavement?"

She contemplated the question longer than was necessary before nodding to my guards. Before they could latch on to help me up, I surged to my feet, standing there loose-limbed, ready to take whatever came my way.

Her eyes widened, lips parted, and the tongue that, just last night, had licked my dick like it was her favorite flavor of ice cream darted out to wet them. Said dick hardened in response. She had the motherfucker trained now. She glanced down, reddened again but damn if I'd apologize. She was mine. My scent was all over her. I'd marked my territory and there wasn't a Wolf or man in the world strong enough to take her away from me. Too bad she hadn't figured that out yet.

Leigh lifted her chin, eyes narrowing when she figured out that I was staring at her mouth. Her tongue immediately stopped teasing her lips. A guy walked up next to her and I almost lost her scent in his. Shit. He was a stew of scents—chili powder, burning tires, gin, plus stale beer and puke. I damn sure didn't want to be in his head. The resentment I got. Rage? What did he have to be that pissed over? Same with why he was exuding indignation. Oh. Wait. I caught a glimpse of a tattoo—the Marine Corps emblem. Yeah, he was probably sure I'd disgraced the Corps, which explained his disgust.

Tough shit.

Hands jerked me toward a waiting squad car. Somebody mumbled their way through the Miranda Rights recitation.

"Do you wish to speak to us at this time?"

"I want my attorney."

That shut things down in a hurry.

🐾 🐾 🐾 🐾

Leigh

I STOOD in the observation room next to Interrogation, watching through the two-way mirror. DPD took over an hour to process Smoke. Brian. No. Smoke. I'd only known him by that name and he owned it, even sitting shackled to the metal desk. He was leaning back in the uncomfortable chair, eyes closed, like he didn't have a care in the world. He could be sleeping for all we knew. The police department mostly used closed-circuit feeds these days but since I knew Smoke, I wanted to be close, where I could see every nuance of his expression.

As he'd requested at the scene, he'd been allowed a phone call. We couldn't question him until his attorney arrived. We were still waiting. The ATF agent standing next to me fidgeted. He'd bristled from the moment he set eyes on Smoke and I couldn't figure out why. He also didn't like me very much.

"Did you fuck him?" the agent growled under his breath.

I jerked my head around and stared at him. "Excuse me?" I could growl too.

"If you have him pussy whipped you might be able to coerce him before his fuckin' attorney gets here."

A plain-clothes cop nodded, obviously eavesdropping. "You're good-looking. Soft. Go work on him, see if you can get him to talk."

They didn't leave me a choice. But I also knew that every word we spoke would be recorded. I exited, slamming the door as I stalked out. Bastards. I struggled to get my emotions under control before I walked into the interview room.

Smoke opened his eyes as a slow grin spread his lips over his teeth. I'd seen that expression on his face before—after going down on me. After bringing me to so many climaxes I'd lost count.

Damn him. Why did he have to be so freaking sexy? And so totally not my type. I didn't do bad boys. Well, except for the romance novels I stashed in my backpack, yeah okay. But real life? They were nothing but heartbreak slapped on chocolate cake topped with whipped cream and salted caramel sauce. They tasted pretty darn yummy until they made your stomach ache. I'd known from the start that Smoke Jenner would do that to a girl—to me—way sooner than later. And now it was sooner. I leaned one shoulder against the wall. I wasn't about to get any closer.

I refused to acknowledge the eyes

watching through the two-way glass.

"Will you tell me why you were at that club?"

"No."

"I can't help you if you don't talk to me."

"Got nothin' to say, babe. I didn't do this."

Lord but I wanted to believe him. Just that morning, I'd awakened in his arms, warm, sated, safe. But the man now staring at me, his face stony, his eyes glinting like topaz jewels? I didn't know him, and my stomach quivered at that realization. Had I ever known him? He was a Nightrider, poster child for the baddest of the bad boys.

And God help me, I was his biggest groupie.

🐾 🐾 🐾 🐾

Smoke

SHE RUBBED her temple and cut her eyes toward the two-way mirror. I wondered who Leigh was staring at behind the glass. Her eyes met mine—a brief flicker of contact. "Talk to me, Smoke. Let me help."

Help? Yeah, right. She'd shown her true colors standing there in that parking lot. I kept my mouth shut. It would take a hellava lot more than her lies to get me to break. I wanted to know what had happened that turned her against me.

"Don't say much, do you?" She looked

aggrieved. I almost laughed. Why the hell was she the injured party? I was the one sitting here in handcuffs.

"What's there to say?" I shrugged. "You wouldn't believe me anyway." And that right there pissed me off. She had no fuckin' clue who and what she was to me, what I was to her. All she saw was the Nightrider patch on my cut. All she saw was the badass biker. I'd never shown her the Wolf. At this rate, I never would.

Someone tapped on the door and she opened it a crack. Then it was pushed open and a tall blonde walked in like she owned the joint. Leigh scowled at the woman. So did I. She was in her mid-forties, and despite the time of night, looked glossy and glamorous.

"Who are you?"

The woman looked Leigh up and down and dismissed her. "I'm Clarice Shepherd, Mr. Jenner's attorney. You had no right to question him without me being present, once he notified you he was exercising his constitutional rights. Now get out. And turn off the video and sound while I confer with my client."

Leigh shot me a helpless look and backed out of the room, shutting the door behind her. Clarice studied me. I studied back. She set her black leather bag on the battered table, reached inside and pulled out a small electronic device. With her back to the mirror, she held an index finger to her lips to shush me.

I hid my grin. That doohickey would not only pinpoint where the bugs were planted, it would emit a pulse that rendered them inoperable. The indicator light flashed four times. DPD was thorough. I braced for the pulse and barely managed to remain stoic. That shit hurt my ears.

Someone next door cursed. Clarice, looking like she belonged on a fashion runway, glided over, braced her very sweet ass on the table next to me and in a soft whisper, asked, "Do you know where the camera is?"

I leaned close so my face was blocked. I wouldn't put it past the bastards to have a lip-reader in there. "Upper right corner. They can't see your face. Can't see mine now."

"Good. My colleague is seeing about your bail. I'll have you out soon and I can guarantee the charges will be dropped by morning. Now, tell me what the hell is going on."

"Club business."

"Shit. The nightclub—"

"No. I'm just down here to take care of Nightrider business. We have nothing to do with that nightclub."

"Not even the locals?" Her lip curled up. Huh. She didn't like them very much which meant she was more likely hired straight out of our National chapter. Good to know.

"Boner's not that ambitious."

"What were you doing there?"

"Saving people."

She scowled at that, but more in confusion than anger. "What? You played hero?"

"Exit doors were chained shut. And there were multiple ignition points."

Clarice stared. Then her lips thinned and her eyes glinted with ice. "Fuckers." She inhaled deeply, showing off her very fine chest to great effect. "The Russian is not going to be very happy about this."

"No shit, Sherlock."

"At least you're smart. You kept your mouth shut and asked for me. Are you ready to get this circus started?"

I nodded, wondering if my ears were bleeding from the subsonic whine. "Yeah."

She flicked the off button with a long, red nail and I breathed in relief. Clarice did her runway-model walk over to the window and tapped on it. Then she leaned in, shifting her face from side-to-side checking her makeup. I choked back a laugh as the door opened.

The first one through was Leigh. She looked pissed. And smelled jealous. My wolf liked that, the bastard. He wasn't all that pissed that she'd betrayed us. The ATF agent, still nursing his hard-on for me, and a DPD detective followed her.

Clarice moved around behind me and stood, a hand on my shoulder. Leigh's eye twitched and the acrid scent of vinegar wafted from her. I schooled my expression, but my wolf was running in happy circles. She was undeniably jealous.

For almost an hour, the cop and the ATF jerk asked questions. Clarice answered for me. Whenever I even twitched like I was going to open my mouth, she squeezed my shoulder. My eyes were almost watering from the vinegar and burnt toast scents swirling in the room.

Leigh was back to leaning against the door and she jumped when someone rapped on it sharply. All eyes went to her and she opened the door a crack. There was a whispered conversation. In wolf form, my ears would have swiveled to hear. In human form, I just listened. Huh. All those witnesses saying I was a hero. How I kicked open chained exit doors. How I carried people out. How I saved their lives. That was the truth, but the woman meant to be my mate would never see that side of me. She saw only the criminal. Whatever.

Leigh came over, unlocked the handcuffs. "You're free to go. For now."

For as long as she lived, I'd never be free. And that sucked donkey balls.

THIRTEEN

Leigh

I KEPT THINGS together through paperwork, angry grousing, and a hurried debriefing. I didn't want to go home. I figured Smoke would be there waiting to confront me and I wasn't ready to face him. Not yet. Maybe not ever. Something inside me curled up in a tight ball at the idea of him not being in my life.

Then I wanted to Gibbs Slap myself for being an idiot. I didn't love the blasted man. I couldn't, given our differences. He was a criminal. Yet, when I didn't see him, the pent-up nervousness inside me threatened to spill out. The times we were together? The sex was over-the-top amazing but there was more. His very presence calmed me, made me feel safe and secure.

Since meeting him, I'd been walking a tightrope and I was so off balance it was just a matter of time before I fell. It would hurt like hell when I hit bottom. It couldn't be real, these feelings. My heart didn't believe the arguments my head kept making. He was an outlaw. There was no way he felt the same way about me. I'd even heard him say he was using me. But.

I scrubbed at my face and looked up at my reflection in the mirror. I'd ducked into the ladies room for a chance to pull myself together. That huge *but* dangled there in front of me like it was a living, breathing entity. The look on his face—betrayal. And a sadness so absolute it broke my heart. And then just that quick, anger and disgust had replaced them.

Nope. I wasn't going home. Smoke wouldn't be there. I was pretty certain of that fact. Walking into my place and knowing his huge presence would never be there again wasn't something I could do at the moment. Besides, there was a fire scene to investigate. Since Smoke was no longer a suspect, I needed to find out who had set the fire—who had set all the fires.

🐾 🐾 🐾 🐾

Smoke

I HITCHED MY ASS on the Harley's seat, legs stretched in front of me and crossed at the ankle. I looked deceptively at ease but the two Nightriders standing in front of me weren't fooled. Lucky Malone, president of the Oklahoma Chapter, was a couple of years younger than me but he sweated Alpha from every pore. Gravedigger Cole was a Wolf I knew well. He was the Russian's favorite enforcer.

"'Preciate the cover, Lucky." Nightriders from the Oklahoma chapter had shadowed me from the other side of the Texas border to ensure I didn't have a tail. I wouldn't put it past the Dallas cops to keep an eye on me. None of them had been happy when I'd been released.

Clarice, the sexy lawyer, had been downright disappointed when she dropped me off at the impound lot to pick up my bike. She'd even picked up the tab for the impound fee. I guess she was hoping to do a trade for services rendered. I wasn't in the mood for pussy and that was a sorry state of affairs. She'd just add the fees to her bill. I'd owe the club big time.

With one short jerk of his chin, Lucky acknowledged the debt. "Brothers take care of brothers."

Yeah, lots of layers in that statement. I glanced over at the big man next to him. "Surprised to see you here, Digger." He just arched a brow. "You callin' me home for church?" Church meant a club meeting—and way too often meant discipline for a brother. I figured my ass was in a sling over the clusterfuck in Dallas.

Digger growled, shoved his hands in pockets, stared at me. "You need church?"

"No. I need to claim my woman and get the fuck out of Dallas."

He stared at me a long time, the expression on his face as readable as a granite block. He spat on the pavement. "Shit." The rest of his words were blocked by the grumbles of the diesel engine on a semi-truck pulling into the truck stop's parking lot. "So that's part of the problem," Digger repeated. "Fuckin' moonstruck." He walked away, a cell phone pressed to his ear.

I sat. Lucky stood, staring down at his boots, rubbing the back of his neck. "Been there," he admitted. "Sucks."

I'd heard he'd mated some time back. "Yeah."

"I found my mate when she was a kid. Had to walk away. Hardest damn thing I ever did. And then I lost her. I figured for good until Fate brought her back into my life." Lucky met my gaze, brother to brother, Wolf to Wolf. "Don't let her go. Whatever it takes. It's worth it."

Digger walked up and I damn sure didn't like the look on his face. "The Russian says we gotta deal with Boner so the answer's no. You stay in Dallas and you stay away from the bitch."

I was damn sorry to hear that. I stood, arms loose at my side but ready for whatever came my way. "I won't leave her alone. You or he will have to kill me first."

Lucky opened his mouth to speak but Digger shut him up with a look. "So it's like that, huh."

Wasn't a question so I just nodded.

"Then get your ass back there, find out who's doin' this shit, claim your mate, and come home."

Sure. I'd get right on that.

🐾 🐾 🐾 🐾

Leigh

TWO WEEKS. I was a basket case and I had no idea why. Which was total bull. I knew exactly why. Smoke. I wasn't eating, barely sleeping, and wasn't anywhere close to solving the string of arson fires. I had a good rep with the department and a better than average closure rate. Even Fielder was giving me the fisheye these days.

A couple of the other investigators convinced me to hit a local hang-out after shift. The place wasn't like a cop or firefighter bar, more metro white-collar than anything, but it was close to our office and the bar food was decent. We talked shop for about an hour and then they got a call out. Good thing they'd only had a beer each. Me? I was about three beers down and decided I'd better get something in my stomach to absorb the alcohol. I could drive. Maybe. I didn't want to take any chances though.

I ordered a burger and fries, with a Diet Coke. I ate slowly and watched the ebb and flow of people. People got up to dance to the jukebox. Others drank. One guy sitting at the bar kept glancing my way. He wore tattered jeans, a waffle-weave Henley shirt, and a leather jacket sporting Italian motorcycle racing emblems. He was cute, if you were into preppy grunge. This place catered to all kinds. I kept eating, sipping my soda through a straw.

After savoring the last fry drenched in ketchup, I figured it was time to face my empty condo. Movement caught my eye and I glanced over to find Mr. Preppy headed my way with a tall glass of dark liquid topped with a lime and a mug of beer.

He set the glass in front of me. "Diet Coke, right? The waitress said you'd gone non-alcoholic." He offered up a cocky grin. "I'm Alex."

Of course he was. He settled into the chair next to me and looked disappointed when he gazed into the empty plastic basket with its minimal smear of ketchup.

"I can order some more," he offered.

"If you're hungry. I'm done, thanks." I pushed my chair back, but he stopped me by draping his arm over the back of it.

"You can't leave yet."

I gave him a slanted-eyed look. "Oh. Really?"

His grin reappeared, offering a dimple as well. "I don't drink diet. I'd hate for this Coke to go to waste." He picked up his mug and held it like he was waiting to clink glasses in a toast. "Besides, I don't know your name yet, pretty lady."

To make this faster, I picked up the glass and took a big swig. "And now I'm leaving."

"Sure you don't want to tell me your name?"

The guy was starting to irritate me. "Look, dude." I waved my hand at my uniform and cocked my thumb at my name tag. "Do I look like I'm here for a hookup?" I gulped down some more of that Coke.

He stared at me and I had the feeling that he was watching for something in my eyes—which made no sense. I gave him a slant-eyed look then stared pointedly at his arm, still draped on the back of my chair. Evidently, my "move it or lose it" glare wasn't very potent tonight. I slipped out the other side of my chair and squirted around the opposite side of the table.

Alex was in front of me and I hadn't even seen him move. I felt weird. Was the room swaying, or was I? I never should have ordered—much less drunk—that third beer.

"C'mon, babe. Let's go home."

Babe. My heart lurched at the word. I glared as Alex's arm came around my waist to support me. He escorted me out through the back exit. Something was off. Wrong. I dragged my feet and tried to call for help but my mouth wouldn't work. Then my legs stopped working. The douche bag picked me up as a black SUV drove down the alley and stopped in front of us. He stuffed me in the backseat. My stomach roiled and I threw up.

"For fucking crissakes." A fist slammed into my cheek and I saw stars...

🐾 🐾 🐾 🐾

Smoke

MY WOLF WENT APESHIT. I was riding down I-635 and the next thing I knew I was wearing furry gloves with claws. He was gnawing on my insides demanding that we get to Leigh. I hadn't seen her since coming back to Dallas. I'd been staying in one of the back rooms at the clubhouse and was currently headed toward a bar. I had a lead on a firebug who liked to copy other people's signatures. I wanted to make sure he wasn't working for the Hell Dogs.

That wasn't happening now. I had to force the wolf down and concentrate on staying human. Leigh was in trouble. I felt it in my gut. I exited the interstate and headed to her condo. She wasn't there. Fuck.

I finally found her POS fire department vehicle parked by a bar a couple of blocks away from her office. She wasn't there. She had been. I questioned the bartender—who saw nothing. I had him by the throat and up against the wall when a waitress walked up.

"She left around eight. Tall guy. Blond. Looked like a college preppy playing dress-up as a bad boy. He bought her a drink." I growled. "Diet Coke with lime. She'd already had three beers with two of the arson guys. They left and she ordered a burger and Coke."

I let the bartender go and focused on the girl. "They go out the front?"

"No. Back alley. It was weird but I was busy. She looked okay—wasn't fighting or anything."

I stormed out the back door, sniffed. Fucking garbage. I caught a whiff of Leigh's scent, and...fuck! Another Wolf. A Wolf I recognized. Motherfucker.

Rook headed me off about five feet inside the front door of the clubhouse. "Smoke." His voice was coated in warning.

"Outta my way, Rook."

"You're a guest, Smoke. And there's not a Blood Moon."

"I'm not challenging the asshole." I wasn't. I'd already called Digger. He was on his way.

"Where is he?"

"He's not here."

No. Boner was fucking in the wind. But someone else was here. That scent was imprinted in my very soul. Pushing past Rook, I stalked to the hall leading to the back rooms. He followed me, wary now.

The hallway reeked with her scent. I stopped, kicked in the door and just stood there, swaying in the doorway. Rage, black and poisonous, slithered through my veins. She lay on her back, the blond motherfucker on top of her. I'd kill the asshole. Kill her. I curled my fingers into my palms to hide the claws erupting from their tips.

My focus narrowed, my gaze arrowing in on her face. Her expression. Those full lips were slack. A line of drool trailed from one corner, a dark spot staining the grubby sheets beneath her cheek. I'd never noticed she slept so damn ugly. My wolf whined, clawing to get out, to get to his mate. Fuck that shit. *His* mate had betrayed us. Again. The wolf growled, straining to reach her.

And that's when I realized. The throb of Leigh's carotid was sluggish. Too slow. What the hell? My boot connected with a bottle as I strode toward the bed. A faint odor drifted up to me. I bent over, snatched the empty.

Holding it under my nose, I inhaled deeply. Wine. Red. Tannins. Wood with spruce berry undernotes. Alcohol. And some chemical I couldn't identify. I traced my tongue over the lip of the bottle, tasted. Figured out what my nose couldn't tell me—roofie.

I launched toward the bed, howling. My wolf wanted to rip the motherfucker's throat out. But my human half couldn't unleash the beast. Not yet. Information. I had to find out why. Find out who. I slammed the dickwad up against the wall.

"Oh yeah, asshole. Awake now aren't you."

"Wha—?" The guy blinked, his expression tinged with stupid.

Scalded milk edging toward scorched hair singed the air. I crinkled my nose to keep from sneezing. The dickless wonder was cognizant now, nervous as shit and starting to panic. I grinned, my canines slightly elongated and I was pretty damn sure red lights flickered in my eyes.

"Why this girl?" I couldn't keep the snarl

out of my voice as my fingers squeezed the guy's throat.

"Orders." The loser shithead choked out the word.

"From who?"

"Can't. Can't rat on brothers."

"You're gonna die either way, asshole. You cooperate, you die quick. Fuck around?" I smiled, scenting ammonia. My prisoner had tipped right over into terror. "I know a man who will take days killing you an inch at a time."

"Boner," he rasped. "Told me if I could get the girl here, do her, I'd get my patch. He gave me the drugs. Told me to have fun." Bravado washed across the man's expression as he suddenly remembered that he was supposed to be a patched-in member of the Nightriders. "And I did. Bitch is full of fun."

I slammed the tool's head against the wall, watched his eyes roll up in their sockets. I stared at Rook and two other Wolves standing behind him. My voice was barely human as I growled, "She's my mate. Tell Digger this one is a special delivery for the Russian."

Rook blanched. "The Gravedigger?"

"Yeah. He's on his way."

My wolf wanted to rip out the kid's throat until I reminded him that our mate was hurt. We'd leave this mess for Digger to clean up.

"Fuck, Smoke. I'm sorry." Rook looked almost as angry as I felt. "We didn't know.

Leave the asshole to us." He handed me a blanket one of the other Wolves had found.

I started to argue but he cut me off. "He's human. And stupid. And did what he thought the club prez wanted. He'll pay for it, Smoke. On my honor. And we'll help Digger with Boner when he gets here."

Wrapping Leigh in the blanket, I cradled her to my chest. I couldn't think about another man's scent on her—in her. I'd go crazy. My driving need now was to get her home. Keep her safe. She was mine, and I was claiming her, even if she denied our connection.

Rook tossed a set of keys to one of the Wolves and ordered, "Go get the Yukon."

"Smoke?" I focused the woman in my arms.

"*Shhh*, baby. Sleep."

"I think I'm punch-drunk."

"Yeah, something like that."

"I missed you." My heart constricted. She sounded so lost. "Are you mad at me?"

"No, babe."

"Sure?"

"Sure."

"Can I kiss you?"

"Okay." With a wonky smile and pursed lips, she kissed me.

My world settled back on its axis.

FOURTEEN

Smoke

LEIGH SLEPT for almost thirty-six hours. Two of the Dallas Wolves got us back to her place—one driving us in the club's SUV, the other riding my bike. Even as pissed as I was, I'd been grateful. She was in bad shape and getting her home on the bike would have been impossible.

She woke up grouchy because I was there. It's like she didn't remember a damn thing from that night. I wasn't sure how I felt about that. She'd passed out on the ride home and remained that way even when I checked her over. The bastard hadn't hurt her, but his scent was on her. Maybe it was better if those memories didn't come back.

"You stay away for two weeks and then decide to just show up? And then you get me drunk?"

"Nope."

"Excuse me?"

"You were already drunk."

"I don't get drunk, Smoke."

"Uh huh."

She threw up her arms, then winced. She lowered her hands to cradle her head.

"What was I drinking last night?"

I needed to tell her the truth, no matter the fallout. "It was two nights ago."

Her head jerked up, her look steely. "What are you saying?"

"What's the last thing you remember?"

Leigh considered. "Work. Three of us went to the Eight Ball. I had a couple..." She paused, rubbed her temples. "Three. I had three beers. I ate." Her forehead crinkled. "A cheeseburger. Fries. Diet Coke. I stopped drinking alcohol." Now she looked puzzled.

"Someone bought you a drink." I worked to keep my voice even. I didn't like leaving punishment in the hands of Rook and his Wolves. I wanted to taste the bastard's blood. No. I wanted to taste Boner's blood.

"Oh. Yeah. A preppy looking guy, only not. He was trying to do this biker grunge look." She looked up, her expression clueless. "Why can't I remember?"

"He roofied you."

Color drained from her face and she stopped breathing. I waited. It took almost a minute before she sucked in air and her face flushed with anger. "What did you have to do with it?"

And here was the tightrope I needed to walk. "Drugging you? Nothing. Finding you and beating the crap out of the guy? Everything."

Her nose crinkled and I wanted to kiss it. "You...rescued me?"

Sort of. "Yeah."

Her expression morphed into one of disbelief. "How did you find me?"

I reached out, snagged her arm and reeled her into my chest. "I can find you anywhere, baby." I whispered the promise into her hair and my wolf settled down. Our mate was safe.

She pushed against my chest. "Wait. Did he…" Her face blanched. I cupped her cheeks and rubbed my thumbs over her skin.

"Shhh. No. I got there in time." Rook had called to say the kid had admitted he didn't penetrate her, that he'd prematurely ejaculated *on* her, not in her. I still had to explain I'd found her naked. "I gotta be honest, Leigh. The bastard was trying. You were completely unconscious. He was stoned out of his mind and having trouble." I had to leash the wolf to keep my claws from erupting. "You were assaulted but not raped." I rasped out the words and she tensed.

"The police…I need…"

"No, babe. I took care of it."

Her eyes widened. "You didn't…" She didn't finish the sentence, but I caught her thought. …*kill him?*

"He's alive." Beat to hell and back but alive. And according to Rook, the kid had learned his lesson. He'd returned to his former life as a frat boy college student. Turned out he was only hanging out for the free drugs and pussy. Little asshole. "He won't ever hurt another woman, Leigh."

"I still—"

"No cops, babe. That's not the way we do things. I took care of it. Took care of you. That *is* the way we do things."

I saw another thought enter her head. "Two days?" she screeched. "I...work...oh crap."

This time I laughed, and it was a relief that I could. "*Shhh.* You've totally lost track of time. Check your calendar." I turned her loose and she wobbled down the hallway to her kitchen. She looked at her watch to double-check the day and time, then the calendar with her days off circled in red.

"*Whew*," she breathed. "I forgot." Then she fixed me with a narrow-eyed glare. "I'm hungry."

🐾 🐾 🐾 🐾

Leigh

SMOKE TOOK ME out to eat at my favorite BBQ place, Red's. It was barely a step up from a hole in the wall but the guy manning the smoker was a pro, they'd never had a health department citation, and you got mountains of meat. I didn't know why I was craving protein, but I wanted those mountains. Ribs. Brisket. Fries. And a sauce meant to be licked off your fingers.

While I stuffed my face, I studied the man sitting across the scarred wooden table from me. I had the feeling Smoke knew more about what had happened to me but just like

I'd known the first time I crashed around him, I was positive nothing horrendously sexual had happened. And it bothered him that I'd been in that predicament. I didn't doubt for a minute that he'd avenged me in his chest-thumping caveman way. He *was* an outlaw biker. And as he'd pointed out, *they* had their own way of doing things.

Beyond that, I also had the sense that Smoke had made it his mission to keep me safe. I should have been freaked out but instead, the idea settled me. I should be on the phone right then calling in a report about my assault. Ignoring law and order wasn't like me. I looked up into his eyes...and got lost. I belonged to Smoke, but he belonged to me, too. I couldn't explain the feeling—or my certainty. Still, I felt it all the way to my soul.

"Take me home, Smoke," I ordered as we left the BBQ joint. "I want dessert." I caught his quick inhalation of breath. Yeah, I knew my biker. He thought he was getting a BJ. I might even give him one after I had a bowl of ice cream.

Smoke

I WALKED through the door and halted in my tracks. Leigh sat on the couch, feet on her coffee table, arms crossed over her chest. I'd cut out before dawn, making sure her alarm was set. Heaven fucking forbid she be late to work. I'd had a decent day. Rook and I met, traded some intel, and I'd tracked down a stray Hell Dog. He was currently sweating bullets in the basement of the Dallas clubhouse. Digger would get the info we needed. And there'd be one less Hell Dog in the world.

Keeping my eye on Leigh, I made note of her sullen expression. What had I done to piss her off this time? "You gonna tell me?"

"Tell you what?"

"Babe."

"Stop doing that."

"Doing what?"

Leigh threw her hands in the air. "You drive me nuts."

"Okay."

"No, not okay, *babe*."

I ducked my head to hide the crooked grin threatening my mouth, knowing it would only piss her off even more. "So...taking a guess here, babe. You don't like it when I do that. Whatever *that* is."

"Exactly."

"Uh-huh."

"*Argh*! You are such a guy."

I glanced down at the obvious bulge in my jeans and then raised my gaze to meet hers. "Babe."

"See?" She sprang to her feet and marched in a circle, her arms flailing. "This is exactly what I'm talking about. You say babe like it...like it explains everything."

"It doesn't?"

"No!"

"So...let me get this straight. I say 'babe,' I'm such a guy, and these two things drive you nuts. Anything else?"

"That's enough for now."

"Good. Now c'mere."

She narrowed her gaze and backed off a step, watching me warily now. "I don't think that's a very good idea at the moment."

"I think it's an excellent idea. C'mere."

"No."

"Babe."

As anticipated, she tossed her hands up, and I moved in before she could do anything else. Circling her body with my arms, I yanked her against my chest and sealed my mouth on hers. She broke the kiss, her hands pressed against my shoulders in an attempt to push me away.

"This is not the way to win an argument with me."

"Babe."

FIFTEEN

Smoke

I WRAPPED my fist around her hair. I was so fucking full of hunger and this little tantrum was too cute. I should tell her what I was, what she was to me. Like so many times before now, I should give her the chance to walk away. But I couldn't do it. Turning her loose would be like ripping my heart out.

A complicated series of expressions clouded her face and I didn't know what to make of them. I should have been able to, given that she was my mate. But she hadn't accepted me, accepted my wolf. Hell, I'd kept him hidden from her.

My emotions were stripped bare. My body was stiff and aching for her. Leigh shivered but before she could push away, my mouth descended on hers and I devoured her. My hands, my mouth—they were everywhere, and totally beyond my control. Touching, teasing, nipping. She arched against me, sucking in air. I was panting hard, but I couldn't seem to get enough oxygen.

I scooped her into my arms and carried her to the bedroom. "Too many clothes," I mouthed against her temple as I put her down next to the bed and set about stripping her naked.

My fingers caressed the skin of her abdomen and with deliberate intent, I nudged her panties down to reveal the thatch of dark hair at the vee of her thighs. Damn straight. I liked my bed partners natural. Bare pubes were just...not sexy. I pushed a finger through her slick pussy then inside her, pushed in a second finger as she moaned. Withdrawing, I laid those fingers against my lips and licked. I enjoyed the fuck out of the way her pupils dilated and her breathing hitched.

"Delicious." Lowering my head, I tasted her with my tongue. I shoved my fingers into her pussy and swirled them around in her slick juices. Pulling them out, I held them to her lips. "Taste."

The skin between her brows puckered and I leaned to press a kiss there. I brushed my fingers across her lips and had to hide my smirk when her tongue took a delicate taste.

"Get on the bed, baby, and spread your legs. I'm going to eat you out."

🐾

Leigh

THE FEW GUYS who'd ever gone down on me did it with little relish. Smoke? He always feasted on me, just like now. And enjoying every lick and nibble. Glorious! I sank my hands into his thick, dark hair. When it seemed like he was never going to stop, I tugged. He ignored me. He speared his tongue into me and then bit my clit. I erupted. Holy volcano, Batman!

His head raised and those intense eyes of his bored into mine. "I'm ready now, baby. I want it hard and rough. You up for that?"

I replied with a slow grin and a sharp jerk of my hands, my fingers still tangled in his hair. He growled—an actual growl that was so animalistic I shivered. He rubbed his chin over my clit and the rough stubble of his shadow beard scraped against my already sensitive skin. The brief pain bled over into pleasure when he started to work me again with his mouth. Then he added fingers and he had to brace his forearm across my belly to hold me in place. I was bucking and screaming and had to keep reminding myself to breathe.

Good grief but this man made me feel things, made me want things. He overwhelmed me. I needed to get away from him. He was so intense, so predatory. But I knew. Deep down. If I ran, he'd chase me, bring me down. Make me his. And I wanted to be his. More than I'd wanted anything in my life. There was something about him, about us. No matter how wrong we were, we fit together so right.

🐾

Smoke

FUCK. I needed to tell her what I was, what she was to me. She needed to meet my wolf. I wasn't completely without honor—not like my old man. He never told my mother what he was. He just got her pregnant and moved on. I was lucky. We lived around the corner from a fire station. One of the firefighters was a Wolf and he recognized what I was. He got me through my first change, mostly kept me on the straight and narrow.

What would Leigh do? I'd finally agreed with my wolf that she was ours. I had to tell her. Had to show her. But what if she walked away? My need for her was too big. She wasn't fertile, thank the gods. Had she been in her cycle, I'd have no chance against the compulsion. I was completely moonstruck, the need to claim her imperative, especially after finding her the way I had. As my mate, she'd be protected. As my mate, there wasn't a Nightrider in the world who would hurt her. I could claim her now and face the consequences later.

I stalked up her body, loomed over her.

"Leigh." I gritted out her name, fighting my wolf for control. "Tell me to stop. Tell me no and I'll walk away." I groaned, trying to get the words out. "I can let you go if you say no, but if you say yes, this is it. You're mine."

Her eyes were glazed with desire and my lust spiked higher. "What's that mean? That we'll be going steady or something?"

I almost laughed, but the sound that

came out more resembled a groan. *Or something* meant so much more than I could explain at the moment. Language and logic were failing me. "Yeah. Or something."

Her slender and oh-so-nimble fingers touched my dick, her thumb rubbing through the cum on its head. "Show me what you've got, big guy."

With a snarl, I jerked her hand away, lined up and pushed into her with a hard thrust. She arched to meet me, eyes focused on mine. I didn't give her a chance to adjust to my size. I couldn't. At that moment, my control was nonexistent.

I pounded into her, imprinting her on my soul, hoping I could do the same to hers. Fuck it. She was mine. Now and always. I clamped my teeth on the thick muscle between her neck and shoulder as I came hard—harder than I ever had.

"Mine." I was still in human form, but it was my wolf controlling my vocal cords. He howled as I started pumping into her again.

I took her three times. Hard. She was all but passed out when I rolled off her, took her into my arms and told her to sleep. A few minutes later, she was sleeping sweet, but I was wide awake.

Then her phone rang.

I've got scars that can't be excised. Not in this life, or the next, I suspect. Fuck all if this woman hadn't gone a hellava long way toward making me forget I wore them. I was fuckin' tired of running from my demons and figured I'd finally found the one woman who believed in me. But she didn't. Not an hour ago I'd fucked us both blind. And deaf. Then her gawddamned phone rang.

"I'm on call," she explained as she pushed me away to answer. She got dressed, cell glued to her ear, so I pulled on my jeans and boots, figurin' I'd need to take her to a fire scene. She ducked out of the room, phone pressed tight, like she didn't want me to hear.

Just nail a stupid sign to my forehead and shoot me. I fell for a fuckin' arson investigator. There's a reason my name is Smoke. You get three guesses why, and the first two don't count.

I stalked her across the room and pinned her against the bar between the living room and kitchen. "Wanna tell me the fuck's goin' on?"

"You lied."

"Never lied to you, babe."

"Really?" The sarcasm in that one word was thick enough to cut.

"What the hell, Leigh?"

"There's been another fire. There's a body. Burned." She looked down, choosing her words way too carefully. "The investigator found the trigger device. It's...one we've seen before. Sort of a *signature*." She crossed her arms, like she was protecting herself. She held out her cell, with a picture on the screen. "Look familiar?"

Yeah. She exuded an odor akin to roadkill. Betrayal? What the fuck? How had I betrayed her? She'd promised my past was my past. I already knew the answer but said the words anyway. "You think I did it."

She raised her chin, eyes blazing. "It's one of your devices."

"Only I haven't made one." I hadn't used any sort of trigger or device that could be traced to me. Not in years.

"Then who did?" More sarcasm and hands fisted on her hips as she glared.

"Good question. One I intend to find the answer to."

"The DA has issued a warrant for your arrest, Smoke. I'm taking you in."

"Yeah? You and what army, babe?"

SIXTEEN

Smoke

LEIGH WOULD BE PISSED once she untied herself. I'd face her wrath after I cleared my name. Did a lot of bad things in my life. This wasn't one of 'em. I'd killed people. Probably hundreds when I was in the Marines. I'd killed for the club—up front and personal. Burning someone up in a deliberately set fire? That was just chicken shit.

Yeah. I'd lost my way right after I was discharged. Too many buddies blown to smithereens. Too much bad shit in the world. I went hunting in my own unique way. The Ghost. What a farce. And I damn sure hadn't been a Robin Hood. I didn't steal from the rich and give to the poor. I took on the dickwads of the world and handed their asses to them. I'd liberated a bunch of Eastern European girls smuggled in as part of the sex trade. I was too stupid at the time to understand the mob and the Hell Dogs had a symbiotic relationship. I sent the girls off and rigged the warehouse to burn.

My problem has always been fire. That shit fascinated me as a kid. I'd start a fire just to watch the flames, to talk to them. All my burns were controlled. I never wanted to hurt anyone. That's how I bumped into Tony, the Wolf firefighter around the corner. He caught me. Taught me. I learned. After that, I was careful. But once I hit puberty, there were a lot of times the guys at the station would catch a glimpse of a stray German Shepherd around fire scenes.

I was seventeen when Tony died in an arson fire. I went a little off the rails but one of the other guys in the station convinced me to join the Marines. So I did. EOD was the perfect fit. Then came my discharge. The Ghost—though I had no clue people called me that. And the Hell Dogs. Those fuckers chased me right into the arms of the Russian, Hardy, Gravedigger, and the Nightriders. I found my family that night. And my reason for being who I was.

In wolf form, I sat in the weeds watching the fire department take care of salvage and overhaul. I needed to get close enough to the body to get a scent. I started with the R&R area. Half the firefighters were taking a break. I crept in, acting skittish. One of them tossed me half a donut. I gobbled it down, eased closer to him.

In ten minutes, I was their new tail-thumping, ready-for-belly-rubs mascot. Yippee. As they rotated back inside the scene, I wandered off, a familiar sight now. The body was bagged and waiting for the ME's van to arrive. I got close enough to recognize the scent.

I immediately recognized a second scent and it hit me like a gale force wind. Leigh. The body was covered in her scent. I tucked tail and ran. I needed answers, starting with the most pressing question. Would she recognize the victim?

🐾 🐾 🐾 🐾

Leigh

I STARED at the face framed by the black plastic of the body bag. Blanching, I locked my knees to remain upright. I recognized that face. Alex. He'd said his name was Alex, and he brought a Diet Coke with lime laced with drugs to my table that night at the Eight Ball.

Still spitting mad that the bastard had tied me up and left, I forced air into my lungs. I had to calm down, but Smoke's words skittered through my memory.

"No, babe. I took care of it."

Worried his definition of "taking care of things" and mine were diametrically opposed, I'd asked him if he'd killed the guy. Smoke had assured me. *"He's alive."*

Only he wasn't. He was dead, found in a burned-out storefront—a fire set using a trigger I knew had been developed by Smoke. I needed to call Captain Fielder. I needed to go to the police. By keeping me from reporting the assault to begin with, Smoke had thrust me right into the middle of this vendetta of his.

I snapped a picture then backed away. I had to find someplace where I could be alone, where I could think things through. First, though, I had a job to do. I'd worry about fall-out and repercussions later. I had a buddy in the DA's office—a guy I'd dated for a while and we'd parted as friends. He was assigned a lot of the arson cases. He liked my closure rate so we worked well together. Yeah, maybe I could talk to David.

Grabbing the rest of my gear, I waded into the scene. A shadow in my peripheral vision caught my attention. A dog—big one. Like a German Shepherd. Something nudged at my subconscious—something about big dogs I'd seen lately.

"Yo, Daniels!" The on-scene arson investigator yelled over at me, breaking my concentration. "About time you showed up."

🐾🐾🐾🐾

Smoke

I STARED at the bottom of the empty glass in front of me. Rook stood behind the bar ready to pour another tequila, but I waved him away. It's fucking hard to drown your sorrows in booze when you can't get drunk.

"Fuck, Smoke," Rook finally said. "This sucks."

"No shit." Boner was in the wind. Digger was tracking him down, but we all knew Boner had been the one to snatch the kid, kill him, and dump him in that building. He'd burned it to make it look like I'd done it. Only I wasn't that fucking sloppy. None of us were. When a Nightrider took out someone, that someone never got found. And how the hell did Boner even know about my past? It wasn't common knowledge, not even among the brothers I was closest to.

Rook lifted the bottle of Patron to his lips to take a swig straight from the source. He never got the chance as all hell broke loose. Stun grenades. Tear gas. Fuck. I couldn't hear a damn thing. I could feel liquid trickling from my ears. Blood. Rook looked as bad as I felt. Neither of us moved as the SWAT team swarmed in.

Three of them took me to the floor. I had to read lips—not that I didn't know the score already. They dragged me outside. Ten more Nightriders were lined up against the wall, held at gunpoint. Digger was there, at the edge of the parking unnoticed by the cops, and he caught my eye. I'd have legal backup as soon as I cleared the booking process.

I went without a fight.

Leigh

I TILTED MY HEAD back as far as it would go against the chair, closed my eyes, and tried to breathe. My chest hurt. My stomach hurt. Even the ends of my hair hurt.

"This is what happens when you drink your whiskey neat," I groused to the empty room. The massive hangover was no one's fault but my own. Coffee hadn't touched it. I'd done the right thing, having Smoke arrested. Every shred of evidence pointed to him. Brian Jenner, USMC. Honorable discharge. Marine Force Recon. Explosive Ordinance Device technician. He could build a bomb faster than he could disarm one.

And he'd told me himself he'd killed people. I pinched the bridge of my nose hoping that would help the pain. It didn't.

What made a man turn bad? He'd been a hero. Had medals to prove it, according to his record. But after leaving the Marine Corps, he'd drifted. Gotten in with the Nightriders. They were…

I felt like I was falling, spinning out of control so I returned my head to a normal position and opened my eyes. The room continued to spin as I stared at the man sitting much too close.

"How the hell did you get out of jail?" I sounded a little to hysterical for my own good.

"And here I thought we were friends."

Even as that drawling, arrogant voice made me jerk my head hard enough to elicit a whimper, tendrils of need curled through my body. How the hell had he gotten inside my house? I'd changed the locks. Oh, wait. Criminal. Great. I could add another breaking and entering to his rap sheet. I was pissed—pissed that he was a criminal. Pissed that he was sitting in my living room. Pissed that I'd second-guessed myself.

Anger. I could use it as a defense. I curled my lip in a snarl. "Not even close."

A slow blink, a quirked mouth. He hadn't touched me, but I was hot for him. "Guess that means we're more."

Wait? "More?"

"Yes, Leigh. More. You think I don't want a relationship? Something permanent?"

"Something permanent? What? Like boyfriend-girlfriend? Marriage? Give me a break, Smoke."

"I plan to give you lots of things, Leigh, but a break isn't one of them."

I forced my brain to think around the headache and the awareness gathering low in my center. He moved closer to me. In self-defense, or maybe it was curiosity, I pushed. "You don't seem the type."

"Type?"

"Yeah, to marry. Someone who would settle down with one woman. You *are* the type who would screw his way through every woman on the planet."

He laughed, the sound like dark chocolate teasing my tongue, and I craved him like he was a hot brownie covered in ice cream. I was in so much trouble.

"What would you say to the fact that when I meet the right woman, I will take her—only her. Now. Always."

"Meet the *right* woman? What, you mean like your soul mate?"

Red lights glinted in the depths of his brown eyes and I wondered how—why—he sometimes seemed so wild, so untamed?

His eyes shuttered and he looked like he wanted to eat me with a spoon. He traced my cheekbone and then my jaw with the tip of one finger. "Something like that."

I closed my eyes as he dipped his head, knowing what was coming but unprepared for the sensation that arrowed through me, from my lips straight to my vagina. He devoured my mouth, sucking, nibbling, invading. He wasn't kissing me, he was conquering me. Words he'd said to me once before came back. *I can let you go if you say no, but if you say yes, this is it. You're..."* As if he was reading my mind, Smoke whispered one word against my skin.

"Mine."

God help me, I was. And I would do whatever necessary to keep him safe.

🐾 🐾 🐾 🐾

Leigh

I WALKED OUT of the courthouse and heard the pipes of a Harley. There's not another sound like it—as I'd discovered during the past few weeks. I didn't want it to be Smoke riding up. He'd done enough damage in my life. My career was in tatters, thanks to his actions. My coworkers in Arson no longer trusted me. Everything I'd worked for was gone in a puff of smoke. No freaking pun intended.

I'd fallen for him—hook, linc, and damn sinkcr. I heard his pretty words and believed them. I surrendered my body to his hands— sexy hands that turned me inside out and set me on fire. I should have known better. He could do no more to me. He'd already incinerated my heart.

Taking the only action I thought I had left, I'd gone to David Ortiz, assistant DA. I laid it all out. The cops already had another APB out for Smoke. Additional charges. My hope was to talk him into surrendering. David had gone to the DA. There was room for negotiation.

The black motorcycle rolled to a stop and the rider sat there, helmet on, watching me through the tinted faceplate. When he removed it, my heart lurched wildly—an unusual action for something that had currently been a lump of charcoal lodged in my chest.

Two deputies, on courthouse security detail, strolled outside. I glanced back at them. Their faces were unforgiving as they formed a line behind me.

"Problem, Miz Daniels?"

"I've got this, deputy."

"If you say so." He didn't sound convinced.

I didn't want backup for this, nor did I need big ears eavesdropping on this conversation so I trudged over to the bike.

"You need to go away, Smoke. They're about sixty seconds away from arresting you."

"Not leavin' without you, babe."

My treacherous heart thudded. "It doesn't work that way."

"Does in my world."

His world. A world of outlaw bikers, shoot-outs, and crazy people. I didn't fit in his world. And he darn sure didn't fit in mine. He was an arsonist and the irony of that made my stomach cramp. It couldn't be that simple.

"Yeah, babe, it is that simple."

How did he read my mind like that? I was a trained investigator. I didn't wear my emotions on my sleeve.

Smoke stared down the guys at my back. "You're comin' with me." He sounded so sure. His eyes flicked to me. "Get on the bike."

I got on the bike. Maybe it was that simple.

🐾

Smoke

HER ARMS AROUND my waist should have settled me, settled my wolf. It didn't. Her scent was off, and I couldn't sniff out her emotions. Weird.

I stopped at a light and swiveled my head to catch a glimpse of Leigh. "Have you eaten today?"

A vee formed between her brows and her mouth drew down at the corners. "No."

That settled at least one thing. I knew where to go. Red's. I needed meat. When I pulled into the parking lot, Leigh didn't seem surprised. I cut the engine on the bike.

"I'm not really hungry."

"Tough shit. You need to eat." I waited for her to get off. When she continued to straddle the bike, I got off and faced her. "What's wrong, babe?"

"Nothing."

I caught a whiff of rotten apples, not that I needed my nose to know she was lying. "Babe."

"Fine!" she snapped. "I've had a bad day, okay? Satisfied?"

Nope. Not even close, but I let it go for now. We'd eat. We'd go to her place. We'd talk. I turned and headed for the entrance. "You comin'?"

🐾 🐾 🐾 🐾

Leigh

SMOKE WATCHED me wearily. The crinkles fanning his eyes, normally put there by a sexy smile, were drawn now by emotions I couldn't pin down. He wasn't angry. Resigned maybe. Or was it regret I saw in his gaze. His face looked drawn and tired.

We'd eaten in silence and then Smoke brought me home. He didn't settle, choosing to lean against the pass-through between my living room and kitchen, his posture wary.

"You're in trouble, Smoke."

His eyes narrowed but he didn't speak—waiting in that patient hunter way of his for me to continue. I pulled out my cell phone, opened my photo library. I tapped the photo I wanted and set it down on the bar. He ignored the phone, holding my gaze instead.

"I recognized him as soon as I saw him. Alex. He was a stupid college kid. He was the one who roofied me. The one you said you'd *taken care of*." I flicked my finger across the screen to reveal a second photo showing the ignition device we'd found at the fire. "This should look familiar too. I recognized it immediately."

"So, I'm guilty as charged?" His voice reminded me of a body in the morgue—cold and lifeless.

"No. But you have to talk to me."

"Not talkin' about this, babe."

I blew out a breath and waited. Silence stretched between us, one so tense a headache was starting, I closed my eyes and tucked my chin against my chest before raising my face to the ceiling. I opened my eyes and shifted so I could focus on Smoke.

"You won't talk, or you can't?" I kept frustration out of my voice because I *needed* to know.

"My life is tricky, babe. The club, it's all about the brothers. We live together. Die together. Betrayal isn't an option."

I unclenched my fists, forced my fingers to stretch. This was not the time to lose my temper. "So...your motorcycle gang always comes first?" Sarcasm warred with hurt, but I had to do something to protect myself. Right? I mean, after everything that had gone wrong in my life because of him, if he picked them over me...

He straightened, eyes as sharp as a hawk's now, his gaze raking me. When he spoke, his voice was deathly cold again. "Club, Leigh. A brotherhood. We aren't a gang." He focused on my face. "Fuck, babe. What did you do?"

Smoothing the hair prickling on my arms, I braced for his anger. "When you picked me up this afternoon at the courthouse? I'd just left the District Attorney's office. I spoke to the DA on your behalf." I lifted my chin. "I made a deal for you."

His reaction was immediate and visceral. "You just signed my death warrant. And yours."

I shivered from the energy emanating from him as nerves propelled me backwards. I knew better than to reach for him so I put a chair between us and shoved my hands into my pockets. "Not true. The DA will protect you."

His howl of laughter wasn't what I expected. Nor was the feral glint in his eyes. "You don't get it, babe. And you never will."

Smoke strode to the door, snagging his leather jacket from the hall tree. He jerked it on over his leather vest. He opened the door, paused. Without turning around, he said, "We're done. Finished. I'll try to protect you before I die."

The door closed with a soft snick. He was gone.

What had I done?

SEVENTEEN

Smoke

I STRADDLED MY BIKE, kicked it into gear. I had to get away. The Nightriders had fancy attorneys, like Clarice. She'd earn her big retainer. She'd take care of the bogus charges. The lawyers always fixed things, even the shit we were guilty of. No, I wasn't running from my arrest warrant. Fuck. I wasn't running at all. I was riding. Heading out into the night where I belonged.

On the road. *Sayonara*, baby. The bitch had turned on me. Again. And I was the biggest gawddamned fool on the planet to have believed we could make something together. Ha. The arson investigator and the arsonist. At best, it was a bad B movie. At worst?

At worst, it was just exactly what had happened. She didn't believe me. Didn't believe *in* me. I was fire. She was water. Only she wasn't. She should have quenched my heat, but *she* was the fire, lighting me up, burning through my blood. She lit up my darkness when she should have just faded into it.

I hit the highway doing eighty. The

wind's fingers twisted in my hair, not like the lover she had always been, but like the whore she could be on a cold night riding down a lonely stretch of road. A more philosophical man might wax on about the symbolism of the empty road. Me? I'd always been a lone Wolf. By definition, I was alone. And who the hell had time to be lonely? Not me. Fuck no, not me.

My heart burned in my chest—not with heat but with a frigid intensity that left my whole body numb. I didn't know where I was going. Didn't care so long as it was away from her. From Leigh. I should never have stopped. Never turned around to go back for her that godforsaken morning.

And I damn sure should never have fucked her. Forget about trust. Forget about love. She was a disaster waiting to happen and when she erupted? She seared me to my very soul. My only hope was to get out of range, so far away she couldn't reach out, couldn't touch me, couldn't set my night on fire.

A Texas State Trooper jumped on my ass at Denton. I was doing 110 miles per hour by Gainesville and the Red River bridge crossing into Oklahoma was nothing but a blur. I'd called ahead. So had the trooper. Oklahoma troopers were massed and waiting, seeing as Texas decided the Okies could take the risk of catching me.

I grinned into the wind, more wolf than man at that moment. With reflexes ingrained in my very DNA, I shifted gears, slammed brakes, slid sideways, and threaded the fucking roadblock like it was the eye of a needle and I was silk thread.

Some of the brothers from the Oklahoma chapter were waiting at the first exit, the one that led to the big Indian casino. I whipped in, rode hard, and got right back on I-35 using the on-ramp on the other side. By the time the cops got untangled, my Oklahoma brothers were strung out behind me, running interference. I grinned, teeth biting at the night when the first set of blue lights lit up the last bike in the pack.

I was running dark, my night vision that of the wolf. The brothers all had their lights on. They'd be picked off one by one, questioned, harassed, but eventually freed. By the time the cops caught the last one, I would be in Oklahoma City at the clubhouse, drowning my stupid, sorry ass in pity and pussy because a Wolf couldn't get drunk. Or stoned. Fuckin' metabolism.

But sex? Yeah. I'd find a willing woman. Or three. Sweet butts who would give me whatever I wanted. And what I wanted was to be free of Leigh. To get her out of my head, off my dick, and the fuck out my life. That was the plan anyway. Too fucking bad I'd already marked her, claimed her.

Leigh

DAY, NIGHT. Night, day. They were all the same. I'd been placed on paid leave pending an investigation. Keeping my job was part of the deal to get Smoke to inform on the Nightriders. If I could deliver suspects or intel on the gang and their cohorts, then those in charge would look the other way about my collusion with a known gang member.

God but I was an idiot. I was so sure that my...my what? My allure? My pure and true love for the bad boy? That my whatever would bend him to my will. What possessed me to believe that Smoke had real feelings for me?

I rubbed my chest, tired of the continuous ache there. My lungs constricted every time I tried to take a deep breath. Tears remained a continuous prickle behind my eyelids. Smoke had never cared for me. He'd lied about his feelings. *Mine*, he'd claimed. I called bullshit on that. I wasn't his. When someone was yours, you did whatever it took to keep them, to hold onto them. You didn't get all pissed and storm out, riding away into the dark with a nonchalant, *"We're done. Finished."*

He didn't care about what I thought, what mattered to me. Law and order. Right and wrong. My freaking job! I'd gambled my heart and ended up losing everything. I'd tried to protect him, to get him right with the law, but did he see that? Noooo. We were soooo done and finished.

The other parting words he said? Those

I ignored. I could protect myself, especially from him. And if his motorcycle brothers were all so loyal, they wouldn't kill him. That was just total crap, justification to walk out on me.

That late-night conversation I'd overheard before we were almost blown up in the boathouse played over and over in my brain. I was just a pawn. Had been from the moment he flashed that cheeky grin at me. He'd obviously been following me, just waiting for a chance to make his move.

It was bad luck that sent that dog running across the road in front of me. That's all. Because no way could he ride around with a freaking silver German Shepherd on his Harley. I paced the length of my living room for the ten hundred thousandth and one times. There was something about that dog.

Ha! That's what I should do. Adopt a dog. Dogs were faithful. They loved you even when you didn't love yourself. They were slobbery and shed and tracked in mud and needed attention. And they took up half the bed. Just like Smoke.

I swiped my cheeks with the backs of my hands. I was *not* crying. I hated him. Period. He'd used me. Set me up. Left me to deal with the fall out. And that witch of a defense attorney was just...mean. I didn't even know why I called her. But I had to try.

All Smoke had to do was cooperate with the DA. He'd get off with probation. We could have moved somewhere, started over. The bitch just laughed at me. Called me stupid and naive. Maybe I was. I curled up on the couch and snuggled Smoke's T-shirt to my chest, burying my nose in it. Leather and hot summer wind and cherry pipe tobacco. It still smelled like him. Barely. Eventually I wouldn't even have that.

I started laughing. I was so damned pathetic. At this point, I should haul my sorry butt off this couch, get in my car and drive to my favorite ice cream parlor. I should buy the biggest Fix & Go container—all fabulous 48 ounces of coffee, cookie batter, and cinnamon ice cream and every single add-in goodness they had.

With that goal in mind, I headed out. Ice cream was my emotional duct tape.

I had to turn off the radio. Every single song was one of those crying-in-my-beer ballads. Where were Garth and Toby when I needed them? I wanted friends in low places, and I'd take them to Honkytonk U for a big party. I pulled into a parking lot to pull up a play list on my phone. I'd plug my cell into the Highlander's sound system, roll down the windows, and sing along at the top of my lungs. That would do the trick.

Once I had things organized, I got ready to pull back into traffic. Except there was fog rolling in. No, not fog. Smoke. I sniffed the air blowing in the window. I'd been a firefighter and now an arson investigator for years. I would never forget that smell. I pulled out on the street and followed the haze.

Three blocks away, I found the fire. An

abandoned two-story building, one side engulfed in flames. I dialed 9-1-1 and gave my report even as I was rushing toward the crowd of people gathering to watch. I needed to make sure they stayed well back, and that no one blocked the street for the engine and truck companies. Then I heard someone yell.

"There's an old man who lives in there!"

I started running.

EIGHTEEN

Smoke

I STARED into the flames lapping hungrily at the wood siding. Fire is a living entity—breathing, all-consuming. It gives life to those in the know and offers death to the unwary. Fascinating. Mesmerizing. Rooted where I stood, I could only watch. I'd smelled the smoke, been drawn inexorably, just like when I was a kid. I was supposed to be with Digger, helping him finish what I'd started. Boner had sold us out. We were all hunting the sonavabitch.

"There's an old man who lives in there!" Someone yelled and figures danced through the flickering shadows.

I heard the shouts, smelled the scorched hair stink rising from the crowd as onlookers panicked. An old man has lived his life. If he didn't have the sense to get out before the inferno burst into being—

A figure detached herself from the darkness ringing the building. She sprinted toward the one entrance no wall of flame blocked. Leigh. And she was headed straight for a hell beyond her imagining.

Three strides. Four. On the fifth, I took

her to the ground, pressed her flat beneath me as she fought.

"Let me go! There's someone—"

"Be still, Leigh."

She froze. "You!"

Not a question. An accusation. I could live with that, but I couldn't live if she died in that building. "Stay here," I ordered. "Promise me!"

I gave her enough space to roll to her side so she could see my face, could see my resolve. "I can't. He could still be alive—"

"I'll get him out, but you have to promise to stay here. Promise. Me!" I gritted my teeth against the need to keep her safe, knowing I couldn't be gentle.

Her eyes searched my face. She relaxed as much as she could, nodded. "Promise."

"No matter what," I pushed. "You stay out here. Wait for the trucks, for the firefighters. Promise me!"

"Yes. I promise. Just...get him out."

I didn't stop to think. Didn't consider the futility. Saving this unknown man was important to my woman, my...mate. I could do nothing else.

I left her with a hurried kiss, charging across the open ground and through that door. Acrid scents burned my nose, my lungs, but I didn't stop my plunge into hell. Seconds turned into days, minutes into weeks, but I found the old man still breathing. I dragged him to the door and outside where the air was only slightly sweeter. I was about to take him farther away when I heard it. A whine, full of pain and desperation.

The old man coughed, spoke. "Momma dog. Pups."

Shit. I left him crumpled on the ground. Returned to the nightmare. I followed the pitiful sound. Found her. A shepherd mix, maybe part wolf. Three pups. I stuffed them in my shirt, grabbed the female by the scruff of her neck with a growl. She stilled as I lifted her into my arms.

The fire breathed around us, hissing and snapping, angry at the intrusion. It reached fiery fingers toward me, brushed against my leather jacket but didn't touch me. Pissed that it had missed, the hellish bitch stretched to the beams above my head. The ceiling collapsed in a shower of sparks, cutting me off from the door. I curled around the dogs. I'd failed them. Failed Leigh. She'd never know how much I loved her.

"I'm sorry, babe."

🐾 🐾 🐾 🐾

Leigh

I STARED as the building collapsed. Sparks shot into the night sky, shooting stars of the most devastating kind.

I'm sorry, babe.

Standing there, frozen with horror, I waited. Smoke would come out. I'd heard his voice. He would walk through the flaming rubble, emerging like the phoenix.

He didn't. Minutes went by. The hose teams from Stations 56 and 20 put water on the fire. A ladder truck arrived. More engines and hoses from Station 22. More water. But no Smoke.

The old transient sat nearby being treated by EMTs. He watched me, his rheumy eyes filled with tears.

"Momma dog and pups," he wheezed. "He went back for 'em."

My throat was too clogged with fear, burned too much from unshed tears to produce speech. My badass biker—the man I hadn't trusted, the one I drove away and ultimately turned my back on because I thought he was a criminal—had run back into a burning building to save a stray dog and her puppies. How could I have been so wrong about him? My heart hurt and I rubbed at my chest. How could I not love a guy like that?

Someone gripped my shoulder, shook me.

"Daniels!"

I looked over at the fire chief. "He's not coming out." I felt dead inside.

"Until we bring out his body, this isn't over."

The chief had far more faith than I did.

I watched, thinking of happier times. Smoke's voice whispered in my memory.

"I know what we can do." He waggled his brows at me.

"I can just imagine," I replied, thinking

his idea would take us into the bedroom.

"You quit, get on the back of my bike, we ride off into the sunset."

So easy, but too late now. The Universe's joke was on me. The arson investigator and the arsonist. Doomed from the start.

🐾 🐾 🐾 🐾

Digger

"HE WENT BACK FOR 'EM," the old man said. Fuckin' fool. The Russian sent Smoke back here to redeem himself. We were going to take out the Hell Dogs attempting to infiltrate our Dallas territory once and for all and we needed Smoke's expertise to bring their so-called clubhouse to the ground. Then his fuckin' hero complex got in the way.

Rook walked up, stood at my shoulder. We both watched, waiting. It'd be a gawddamned miracle, but Wolves were tough, and Smoke was tougher than most. Still, we were here on business. I jerked my head toward the crowd. Rook nodded and we split up to mingle with them.

I got a chance to talk to the old guy when Rook arranged for a distraction and the EMTs took off to check the woman who'd fainted.

"You're like him," the man rasped. "The one who started it." That got my attention. The dude's fingers scrabbled at my cut. "His said president. He set the fire. I tried to stop him. He pushed me down. Don't remember anything after that, not 'til that young feller dragged me out."

Fuck. Boner. Had to be. I signaled Rook and we took off. Smoke was on his own. For me? It was time to hunt.

🐾 🐾 🐾 🐾

Leigh

THE RISING SUN painted the eastern horizon in pale imitation of the fitful fire still burning. The building was a total loss. And I was a total wreck. An ambulance stood by just in case. Just in case Smoke walked out of what had been an inferno. Just in case the firefighters currently poking through the debris found his body.

My eyes felt like burning embers had been embedded in my lids when I rubbed them with the heels of my palms. No tears. They'd dried up hours ago. A firefighter from Station 22 walked up, stood beside me, silently watching the salvage and overhaul—only there was nothing to salvage.

"You should go home, Leigh."

"Can't. Not until I know for sure."

"The captain got a call from the hospital. The old man is gonna be fine."

"Good. That's good."

"C'mon. You need coffee. Red Cross is here."

He herded me toward the canteen truck parked next to the R&R area set up for the firefighters and several already stood in line. Others sidled up behind us.

"Who bought it?"

"Supposedly the asshole who set the fire. Serves the sonavabitch right."

I pivoted to confront the callous bastards—two cops stuck on guard duty and pissed about it. Before I could retort, a shout from the ruins had hope surging.

"Get the EMTs!"

I raced back, watched a man emerge. My heart clogged my throat and I couldn't breathe. I stared, inching closer. But it wasn't Smoke. Somebody else. Holding his arm like it was broken. It would never be Smoke ever again. I had to accept he was gone. And my heart fractured.

NINETEEN

Digger

I GLANCED DOWN. The silver and black wolf at my side watched the activity below, his nostrils flaring at the acrid scent of wet ashes. My own nose did the same. That shit stank. The woman—though it was hard to tell she was female given the coveralls—holding his attention stood ramrod straight while staring at the burned-out husk of the building.

Dropping my hand to his back, his ruff bristled. "Time to go." He stared up at me then turned and lunged to place his paws on the side rails of the borrowed truck, *whurfling* softly to the dog curled up in the pickup's bed. "She's fine. So are her pups. We'll take care of them, but we need to get out of here."

Opening the passenger door, I waited until he jumped into the seat. I couldn't help but wince at the missing patches of fur and scorched flesh along his chest and wrapping across his left shoulder, back, and flank. Burns hurt like hell even if you were a Wolf.

I made sure the mama dog and pups were secure as I rounded the back of the truck to get into the driver's seat.

Digger? My name echoed in my head.

"Yeah?"

I can't leave her.

He wasn't talking about the dog. Fuck. "You can't stay."

Silence.

I glanced over. His gaze was fixed out the windshield. He'd always been strong, as evidenced by his ability to speak the way we were. It wasn't easy, especially for a lone Wolf. Not many of our kind ever developed the ability. It was one reason why the Russian could send him all over the country. Still, it didn't fucking matter how strong he was. This separation—the knowledge he couldn't be with her—would kill a lesser Wolf. And it would likely cripple him in the long run. I knew all about that.

He howled his lament as I put the truck in gear. The windows were rolled up but that heart-breaking sound couldn't be contained by steel and glass. As if she'd heard, the woman down below turned a tear-streaked face to the sky. Driving away, I knew I'd ripped out Smoke's heart.

And I couldn't do a damn thing about it.

🐾 🐾 🐾 🐾

Leigh

I STUDIED the hole in the interview room's wall. Vaguely oval. About the size of my hand. I wondered who'd put their fist through the sound-proofed sheetrock. The door opened and a DPD detective walked in with the fire marshal, Chief Wilson, and the guy from ATF. "I'm Detective Bob Evans, Ms. Daniels." He said.

"Sergeant Daniels." I corrected the detective automatically. Except I probably wasn't a sergeant any longer.

"Look, Leigh, I know this is hard, given your connection to the suspect."

Hmm. Using my first name to establish a connection. I wanted to laugh. This whole idiotic scene was straight out of Interrogation 101. I'd already passed this course with flying colors.

I leaned forward on the table, my expression as sincere as I could make it. "Look, Bob, you have no clue if this is hard or not. Let me explain something. We aren't going to be BFFs. Good cop, bad cop won't work on me. I'm not a person of interest. If you stretch the truth, you might convince a judge I'm a material witness."

Chief Wilson, the fire marshal, cleared his throat. Technically, he was in charge of the Arson squad and my superior. "Leigh, just a few more questions. You keep telling us Brian Jenner is innocent."

"He is." A dull headache throbbed between my eyes. I felt adrift and I'd bet my eyes looked glazed over. I corrected myself. "Or was. Since he's dead."

"We haven't found his body, hon." Detective Bob was still playing the good ol' boy. "When was the last time you saw him?"

"That was the last time, *hon.*" I pressed the heels of my hands to my eyes as the sting of tears I didn't have left to shed burned. "He brought out the old man then went back into the fire to save the dogs."

"A man like that doesn't save stray dogs." The cop was scoffing now.

"You don't know what kind of man he is. Was." I stood. "We're done. *I'm* done. Smoke Jenner is dead. It's over. If you're going to charge me with something, then get on with it. I'm through answering questions."

I'd learned Smoke's lesson too late. Loyalty was important. I finally recognized what he'd been saying all along. I'd betrayed him and yet he'd stayed loyal to me, stayed to protect me. And he'd died because of it. The *what ifs* were tearing me apart.

The men exchanged looks but no one spoke. I let the silence stretch then said, "Since I'm not under arrest, outta here."

None of the three men in the room attempted to stop me. The door wasn't locked but I paused for a moment, fitting my hand over the hole. I knew now what would drive someone to put their fist through a wall. They would do it to feel. Something. Anything. Because even pain was better than the numbness.

TWENTY

Digger

EASY AND I had ridden down from Kansas City to preside over the Blood Moon challenge. A couple of out-of-towners and wannabes showed up. Rook was a quiet Wolf—the total opposite of Boner. Motherfucker. If Boner hadn't died in that fire, it wouldn't have taken us as long as it did to track down the whole ugly mess. The cops found what was left of his body in the rubble. They had to do fuckin' DNA tests by grinding up his teeth, which was bad for the Wolves. His fucked-up genes would put us on the black hats' radar.

None of the Dallas chapter brothers wanted to challenge Rook so that left the outsiders. Easy and I were there to make sure things stayed fair. Rook was strong enough to take on any comers. We represented the national council because whoever won would have to get the Russian's approval. That didn't come easy. Rook took the presidency without shedding any of his blood. That said something. We handed over the President's cut with the Russian's blessing.

A month after that last fire, the Nightriders took out the Hell Dog compound with the help of a Wolf Hardy knew from his Army days. Boomer walked the straight and narrow except when it came to threats to his pack. For some weird reason, that group of ex-military Wolves considered the Nightriders as an extension of their pack. The Russian extended the courtesy in return. We'd worked together on a couple of things—involving Hell Dogs and those bastards from Black Root Corporation. We wouldn't have known about them if not for Boomer and his Alpha, a former command sergeant major named Mac McIntire. We'd had a powwow with them, and McIntire's crazy-ass mate, Hannah.

I hadn't caught Black Root's stench here in Dallas. That meant jack shit. Those assholes were cockroaches. You never saw them until you snuck in and turned the lights on. Then they scattered like the dirty buggers they were.

Easy insisted we check on the woman who would have been Smoke's mate before we headed home. He'd gotten soft, being mated and living with his and Sam's adopted kids. Still, it probably wouldn't hurt. If things had been different, the woman would have been part of our pack. Four months was enough time for her to move on.

Rook, for some reason, had kept tabs on her. She'd served her suspension but didn't return to the arson squad. Instead, she was filing paperwork at the fire academy. Easy and I tracked her down there, then followed her home. Four months ago, she'd been healthy, vibrant. And I'd seen her devastated that morning after the fire. Now? She was nothing but a shadow. She'd lost weight and her eyes were darkly bruised. Shit.

"Fuck, Digger. What are we gonna do?"

Good question. I didn't have a fucking answer.

"The mating bond..." Easy's voice trailed off and I caught a hint of pain there. His mate had ignored their bond at first and things went to hell in a hurry in the aftermath.

"Yeah," I agreed. Easy stripped down. "What the hell?"

"I'm shifting. She'll let me in. You come knock on the door, looking for your lost dog. We'll play it from there." The bastard gave me a cocky grin and changed. Moments later, a black and silver wolf with Siberian husky eyes *whrfled* at me, wagged his tail like a fucking dog and trotted across the parking lot.

🐾 🐾 🐾 🐾

Leigh

I NO LONGER CARED what happened. There was a huge, gaping hole in my chest where my heart had once been. I'd always thought my girlfriends were drama queens when they carried on after a break-up. Their rhetoric was hyperbole at its silliest. Then I'd met Smoke. Only we hadn't exactly broken up. Smoke was gone. Dead.

I didn't eat. I didn't sleep. I didn't do

anything but sit and stare and nurse the hurt that ached all the way to my soul.

Yeah. No hyperbole here. None at all.

When I heard the scratching at the door, I opened it. Idiot that I am. A beautiful husky sat there. As soon as the door was wide enough for him to dart in, he did. He sat in front of me, whined, and pawed at my thigh. He was huge for a husky and I wondered if he might be a wolf mix. He had incredible blue eyes and they looked...right through me, like he *knew* the agonized misery I lived with every day.

Sinking to my knees, I buried my fingers in his fur. He licked at my tears and I briefly considered keeping him. Which was stupid. I couldn't take care of myself. There was no way I could take care of a pet. Except he didn't look like a stray. Someone in the complex had probably lost him. Two minutes later, someone cleared their throat. I hadn't closed my door. My mistake.

TWENTY-FOUR HOURS LATER, I was still attempting to figure out why a couple of very big and very scary bikers had dragged me to this derelict train depot outside of Kansas City. The fence around the place made it look like a prison, except I could see the original building. It had probably been beautiful once. All Art Deco granite and interesting architecture. Which just went to show how brain dead I'd become. I was probably here to die, and all I could think about was how someone should restore the building.

They were Nightriders. Something Smoke had said to me before he left kept playing in my head. *You just signed my death warrant. And yours. I'll try to protect you before I die.* I'd blown it off as his way of making a dramatic exit. Now, I wasn't so sure. But why had they waited so long? A month after Smoke's death, there'd been a big explosion that leveled a compound allegedly belonging to the Nightriders' archenemies, the Hell Dogs. No bodies were ever found— dead or alive.

Smoke hadn't betrayed his so-called brothers. That whole deal with the DA had been on me anyway. My guess was they were bringing me here to find their brand of justice. Fine. I was dead inside. If they killed me, it would just mean that my body had finally caught up.

The black Yukon we'd ridden in coming from Dallas paused at the gate. Two guys gave me steely-eyed stares. They could double as executioners for all the emotion they showed. Three men had ridden in the Yukon with me. Two more followed on Harleys. I must be really scary.

The vehicle rolled to a stop near the building's entrance. The guy who'd appeared at my door and the guy whose eyes reminded me of that damn dog's got out. They spoke briefly with the two motorcycle riders. Then my door opened. I was hauled out, the two men climbed in, and the Yukon left.

Scary Man and Blue Eyes deposited me inside a big room—probably what had once been the station's lobby. Three men stood there waiting. Vaguely aware of probably 30 more people in the room, my attention was caught and held by the man in the middle of the unwelcome committee. He was tall, broad-shouldered and incurably handsome. He also looked like he could snap me in half. He spoke to Scary Guy.

"Are you sure this is the right thing?"

He sounded foreign and I worked to place the accent. They all stared at me as if waiting for me to speak. I kept my mouth shut, studying them. The foreign dude was in charge. I didn't need the "President" patch on his vest to know. Power rolled off him.

The two men standing at his sides were almost as big. The one with the vice president patch stood at attention, like a soldier. The other was leading-man handsome. What was it about these bikers? Every last one of them was the stuff of romance covers. The sexy beast with the Russian accent gave me the once over. Twice. No one spoke. He approached, stared down, holding my gaze.

"You are Leigh Daniels."

It wasn't a question so I didn't answer. My knees were going rubbery and my insides felt like they were turning to liquid. This was undoubtedly the scariest man I had ever seen in my life. And despite my earlier musings, my sense of self-preservation was kicking in big time. Turns out I wasn't quite ready to die after all.

"Do you know why you are here?"

I shook my head, not trusting my voice. I wanted to turn mouse and hide, and I was pretty sure anything I said would come out in a squeak.

"Have you seen Smoke's wolf, Leigh Daniels?" the Russian asked.

"Smoke's wolf?" Now I found my voice, though I was completely confused. "I don't know what you're talking about."

He snapped his fingers. "Easy."

Blue Eyes stepped around me and stripped. I watched, mouth hanging open. Then the man disappeared, my embarrassment at his rampant male nakedness replaced by a cringing wonder as bones snapped and muscles twisted. In the man's place stood...not a dog, as I realized too late. He...it was too wild, too beautiful to be a dog. Black, silver and white with eyes of Siberian husky blue. I'd buried my fingers in this animal's fur but at the moment, he looked like he would bite first, bark later. This was definitely not a dog. This was a wolf. In all his wild glory.

My knees collapsed and I sat on the floor. The wolf was so big I couldn't meet him eye-to-eye. He was a head taller as he sat there, panting a little. How had I not noticed that before? And how was this even happening?

"Drugs." Had to be. They'd roofied me or

something. I muttered the word but the men around me laughed and the wolf made a sound too much like laughter for comfort.

"No," the Russian said. "We did not drug you. But now you know our secret. Smoke's secret."

Werewolves? Not possible. They didn't exist. Not like this. The man with the vice president patch squatted beside me. He was just as hard as the others but there was a tiny flicker of compassion in his eyes.

"We're Wolves," he said, as if that explained everything. "We aren't quite human." Well d'uh! My expression must have given my thoughts away because he continued. "We are genetically similar, but we carry a splice in our DNA, an extra gene that allows us to shift.

"Can you accept Smoke as this?" The Russian's voice was deep, with a growl overlapping the words.

A tear trickled down my cheek. I didn't know. This was...too much. Too fantastical. None of it made sense. Why would it matter? Smoke was dead.

"He's dead," I murmured, as much to myself as to them.

"No," the Russian said. "He is not."

My heart stopped and my head jerked up on its own. I stared at the man, scarcely daring to believe him.

"Alive? Smoke is alive?" I surged to my feet with new-found hope. "But...I was there. I saw."

"He survived the fire," the really scary guy who had kidnapped me said. "I brought him here."

"Without you, he is only half a man. One who lives in shadow," the Russian continued. "He is not as he was. Are you ready to accept that?"

Since I had no clue what he was talking about, I kept my mouth shut. Was this all some elaborate joke? And what did he mean that Smoke wasn't as he'd been? I blinked, putting the Russian's words together. Half a man. Was Smoke caught in some nightmarish half-form like in the movies? Was that what he meant about me being able to accept Smoke as...a wolf? *Without you...* My mind whirled, sorting memories. Mates. His other half. Smoke's words came pouring into my heart. He'd thought I was asleep when he said them. *Mine*, he'd promised. *Forever.*

"Be sure, Leigh Daniels, or leave."

My brain went blank. This...it was all too much. I couldn't process the information. Werewolves. Smoke alive but not. I stared at the wolf still sitting in front of me. Horror welled up until I thought I would vomit from it. I left. Not running. Stumbling.

I got as far as the gate then stopped. I told my foot to step forward, but it refused to obey. The gate stood open, the guards invisible. I was steps from freedom, but my body would not move. My heart pounded in my chest. I couldn't breathe, couldn't see for the tears streaming from my eyes. Blind and in agony, I sank onto the damp ground, hugging my arms around my chest.

A hand settled with utmost care on my shoulder. Hands lifted me to my feet.

"Go to him." The Russian, his voice unbearably gentle. "If you leave him, we will lose him to the beast." Now he sounded unbearably sad. How could a man so hard and ruthless before now be this...caring protector?

These were Nightriders. Outlaw bikers. They were hard, cold. Killers. They didn't get to care, to be compassionate. Yet I could see it on their faces. Smoke mattered. Smoke—brothers, he'd called them. I saw it now, in their eyes. They mourned him and not because he'd died, but because he was lost to them some other way—a way I didn't understand.

I bent over from the waist, struggling to breathe. I closed my eyes, opened my heart, my mind. Smoke. He wasn't far away but he was. I tried to touch him, didn't realize I was stretching out my hand, that I was walking toward the center of the compound until I blinked. I stopped.

None of the men spoke. Skin was drawn tightly across their faces. I recognized exhaustion in each of them. I still didn't understand any of this, but it didn't matter. Nothing mattered except seeing Smoke. Touching him.

They must have seen something on my own face because after a nod from the Russian, the big guy who'd kidnapped me marched me to a second building behind the depot. The others trailed behind, entering the barracks-style building with us. Down a hallway of identical doors and then we stopped. Without knocking, the man opened a door, shoved me in, and retreated.

A figure stood in the shadows. My heart hammered. I knew this man. I knew his size, his shape, his smell. "Smoke." I breathed his name then I was in his arms.

I angled my head, found his mouth. He kissed me, our breath mingling like a shimmering bridge between reality and dreams, shadow and light. Was he truly real?

"Yes. Are you?"

We were on the bed, heart-to-heart, mouth-to-mouth, our bodies aligned like Jupiter and Mars. I wanted more than just arousal. I wanted the intimacy of joining with him, the unity of our souls as we came together. I wanted only him. Clothes disappeared and finally, finally, I pulled him into the aching heat of my body. He groaned. I sighed.

Yes, I decided. I was totally ready.

TWENTY-ONE

Leigh

LATER, AFTER MAKING LOVE a second time—and again after that, I lay with my head on his shoulder. The room remained shadowed and I had to use my fingers to *see* him. I found the ridges, the pebbled skin, the scars left behind from horrific burns.

"Aren't you going to ask?" His voice rumbled beneath my ear. I shrank away from his question, from my own.

The Russian's words came back to me: *"He is not as he was. Are you ready to accept that?"*

Despite what I'd said standing there at the gate, I wasn't ready. Just like Smoke wasn't ready to face me in the light. "You're alive. That's all that matters."

"Is it?"

I pushed up, drew my knees in so I was kneeling beside him. He was masked in shadows, all but his eyes. Those were alive, vivid enough to cast their own light.

"Am I a prisoner?" Nothing like going on the offense to change the subject.

"What do you think?"

"I think I was kidnapped by Nightriders,

brought here by force, and…" I trailed off.

"Thrown to the monster?"

Smoke always could read my mind. Damn him.

"You're supposed to be dead. Four months and not a word from you."

"And you're supposed to love me." His voice cracked. "Come hell or high water."

I dashed tears from my eyes. "No, you don't get to hold that over me." Even as I argued, I wondered how he would ever be able to forgive me.

He kissed me, murmured, "I already have."

The pressure in my chest eased and I inhaled deeply. Though it was morning, he'd refused to open the curtains or turn on a light. My fingertips again traced the damage the fire did to his impossibly beautiful body. "Then let me see."

Smoke stiffened and he bit back a growl. The hair on my arms prickled as the power of his wolf roiled beneath his skin. In between our lovemaking, he'd talked about being a Wolf, about the animal who lived in his soul. A light bulb clicked on.

"If you won't show yourself, show me your wolf."

Time hung suspended. Neither of us dared breathe. Then he rolled away, stood beside the bed and time snapped back into being. He made no verbal sound as sinews stretched, bones popped, and muscles twisted with a wet sound. Then I was looking at the most beautiful wolf I'd ever seen. He was...magnificent. A silvery gray with black markings, he watched me through golden brown eyes. Through Smoke's eyes.

I surrendered to the need to touch him. I slipped off the bed and wrapped my arms around his neck, his fur absorbing my tears. He was a beast, but he was my beast. I loved him.

I love you too, babe.

Smoke

LEANING MY SHOULDERS against the wall, I bit the insides of my cheeks to keep from smirking at her. Leigh was so damn easy to play. She whirled at the end of the hallway and marched back past me, for the twentieth time, repeating her action at the opposite end. This time, when she drew even with me, I snagged her arm and reeled her in, securing her against my chest with both arms around her waist.

"You're making me dizzy, babe."

"I want to know what's going on over there. I mean, seriously? What are they doing? Deciding whether we live or die?"

Chuckling, I wheezed a breath. My lungs still hadn't healed completely from the fire. "Well, close."

She thumped my shoulder. I wasn't quick enough to hide my wince from her. My lungs weren't the only thing that hadn't completely healed. Her face morphed into an expression of concern. Her fingers hovered over the spot, tentative.

"I'm sorry. I didn't mean—"

"It's fine, babe. Burns heal slow. Even for us."

Now she looked dubious. "Yeah...about this whole werewolf thing."

I curled my lips between my teeth and stared at my boots to keep from laughing. "We've discussed this, babe. We don't say the W word." She rolled her eyes and I did laugh then. Something opened in my chest. I'd spent most of the past four months as a wolf, curled up in the dark, avoiding my brothers. But this remarkable woman had returned to me, bringing light and laughter back into my life. She'd been here a week and the other mates had taken things into their own hands.

Love you, babe.

She stared at me. "What did you say?"

"You heard me."

She blinked rapidly. "No. Not exactly."

Sure you did.

Her mouth dropped open and I grabbed the opportunity to kiss her. She pushed against me, breaking the kiss. "Your lips didn't move." Her eyes were narrowed, her gaze accusatory. "Are you in my head?"

Of course I am. Just like you're in mine.

Accusation morphed into suspicion. *I call bullshit.*

"Babe. I'd never bullshit you."

"Stop that!"

I laughed again and yanked her to my chest, kissing her until she stopped fighting me. The mates picked that moment to burst through the Barracks door. The party was starting.

🐾 🐾 🐾 🐾

Smoke

WELL AFTER MIDNIGHT, the party was still going strong. We'd slipped away and now stood next to my bed, side-by-side, arms and bodies stiffly straight. The party in the clubhouse had spilled over to the Barracks as my brothers found their bedmates for the night. I listened to the noise outside my room then turned my head as Leigh turned hers. We grinned. And dove onto the bed.

She laughed as I ripped her T-shirt down the middle, then she groaned as I nipped first one bare breast then the other. Gasping, she let out a shrieking giggle as I kissed my way down to her jeans.

"I hope this isn't a favorite pair," I said, claws sprouting and slashing through the denim. I had her naked but for my cut in just over a minute. Before the night was over, I'd have her from behind, still wearing the cut so I could read its PROPERTY OF SMOKE rockers.

"Not fair," she complained. "You have too many clothes."

Good thing I could multitask. Except I hesitated as I reached to pull my T-shirt over my head.

"No," my mate said. "Don't stop. You are perfect to me."

After that instant of self-doubt, I stripped and jumped back into things. We had fun, teasing each other. We were silly and foolish. Making love as true mates painted our deep desire with bright splashes of color.

My hands were everywhere. Her greedy mouth tasted me. Reckless, we rolled and chased each other across the bed. I ate her pussy like a starving man, driving her up and over. She laughed from sheer pleasure, her fingers entwined in my hair, pulling and tugging, as she tried to control me.

This, I thought. This is what mating meant. The unity. The pleasure, the sheer adventure of having this woman in my heart. She amused me. Enchanted me. Owned me. She was the one thing I'd searched for my entire life—my other half.

I slipped up her body, entered her on a gliding thrust. Her eyes, glowing almost as bright as mine must be, stayed on mine. Fuck. I loved this woman—Leigh—with every cell of my body.

She reached up, stroked my cheek. "I see him," she whispered. "The wolf. And I see you."

My wolf settled. *It's good to have a mate*, he told me.

Leigh's lips curved as I lost control and

spilled inside her. She fell over the edge with me a heartbeat later. My forehead rested on hers and she lay under me, limp and satiated.

"Wow," she sighed, "That should do it."

I kissed her and pumped my hips. "Then we're definitely doing it again."

"Beast," she complained, still smiling.

"As long as I'm your beast."

Forever, she said.

Outside, a bonfire danced in the fire pit as my brothers enjoyed the party, but the flames didn't draw me. Not any longer. I kissed Leigh, long and deep. She was the fire that lit up my night now.

"Forever," I promised.

🐾 🐾 🐾 🐾

Dear Reader:

I have a not-so-secret love of MC books. There's just something about finding the protective side of a really bad alpha male. When the world of my Moonstruck Wolves, detoured into the gritty and oft-times violent lives of the Nightriders, I happily jumped on for the ride. These outlaw MC brothers thundered out of the dark into my imagination, and above the roar of their Harleys, they introduced themselves.

I had other plans for Smoke, and he derailed them almost immediately. As a result, his story had to wait awhile. Leigh, his heroine, is exactly who I wanted her to be. Luckily, Smoke had no complaints. Stories set in this world won't be for everyone. The Nightriders are an outlaw motorcycle club. Their enemies think nothing of rape, torture, and murder. If readers are sensitive to these themes, this is not the series for them.

Thank you for visiting my worlds. The door is always open so don't be a stranger. Happy reading!

~Silver James

Thank you for reading this book!

Reviews and word of mouth help other readers find books to read. I appreciate every review. Please consider leaving one on Amazon, Goodreads, and/or on the book review site of your choice. If this is your first Nightrider book, please check out my other stories in this series as well as the books in my Moonstruck world, my Urban Fantasy series Penumbra Papers, or my sexy contemporary series from Harlequin, Red Dirt Royalty. Keep reading for the list of all my titles.

TITLES BY SILVER JAMES

Paranormal Romance

MOONSTRUCK WOLVES

In the beginning, there were the Wolves of Army Special SciOps Unit 69...

Moonstruck Genesis:
Moonstruck: Secrets
(Contains the books Blood Moon and Bad Moon plus additional chapters and cut scenes)
Moonstruck: Lies
(Contains the books Hunter's Moon and Wolf Moon plus additional chapters and cut scenes)
Coming soon:
Moonstruck: Betrayal
Moonstruck: Retribution

Moonstruck:
*Blood Moon – Book 1
*Bad Moon – Book 2
*Hunter's Moon – Book 3
*Wolf Moon – Book 4
*Bride's Moon – Book 5
*Rogue Moon – Book 6
*Christmas Moon – A Moonstruck Novella
(#7)

Series set in the Moonstruck World:

Welcome to the darkest side of the Moonstruck world. Not every Wolf walks the straight and narrow like the Wolves of the 69th. Gritty, earthy, and violent, rogue Wolves run on the criminal side of society. Gun running, strip clubs, bounty hunters, the Nightriders live their lives in the outlaw 1%. There's sex, violence, and violent sex, and sometimes, a Wolf smacks up against the woman destined to turn him moonstruck...

Nightriders MC
Night Shift – Book 1
*Remember the Night – #1.5
Night Moves – Book 2
Night Fire – Book 3
Night Fall – Book 4

Other Books set in the Moonstruck World:

Susan Stoker's Worlds
**Rescue Moon
**SEAL Moon
**Assassin's Moon
Under the Assassin's Moon

Elle James Brotherhood Protector World
**Montana Moon

Moonstruck Wolf
**Blood & Fire (revised)
**Crash & Burn (revised)

Urban Fantasy

PENUMBRA PAPERS

That Ol' Black Magic
Season of the Witch
The Devil's Cut
The Sound of Silence

Contemporary Romance

From Harlequin Desire

Red Dirt Royalty

Cowgirls Don't Cry
The Cowgirl's Little Secret
The Boss and His Cowgirl
Convenient Cowgirl Bride
Redeemed by the Cowgirl
Claiming the Cowgirl's Baby
The Cowboy's Christmas Proposition
Billionaire Country
RDR #9 coming May 2010

From Wild Rose Press:

Time Travel Paranormal

Faerie Reign
Faerie Fate
Faerie Fire
Faerie Fool
*Faerie Reign
(Digital 3-book boxed set at a special price)
*Faerie Faith (Twelve Brides of Christmas)

Contemporary Romance

Class of '85 Reunion Series:
*Fairy Tales Can Come True
*Promises, Promises

Dearly Beloved Series:
*Best Laid Plans

Paranormal Noir

Other Novella:
*Café Midnight
(Paranormal Noir Mystery)

*Available in digital format only

**Books previously published in worlds created by other authors that have been, republished under a revision or reassignment of rights

ABOUT THE AUTHOR

Silver James likes to take walks on the wild side and coffee. Okay. She loves coffee. LOTS of coffee. Warning: Her Muse, Iffy, runs with scissors and can be quite dangerous. She's the author of four award-winning series: Nightriders MC, Moonstruck, The Penumbra Papers, and Red Dirt Royalty. She's been a military officer's wife, mother, and has worked in the legal field, fire service, and law enforcement. Now retired from the "real world," she lives in Oklahoma and spends her days at the computer with two Newfoundland dogs, the cats who rule them all, and the myriad characters living in her imagination. She writes dark paranormal romantic thrillers, urban fantasy, and sexy contemporary romance for Harlequin Desire.

To find out more about Silver and her books, visit her website at **www.silverjames.com** where you can sign up for her newsletter, get info on all her books, and other fun things. You can also track her down (and follow her!) on Facebook at Silver James Romance, Instagram at Author Silver James, Twitter at @SilverJames_, and Pinterest at Silver James.

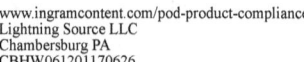